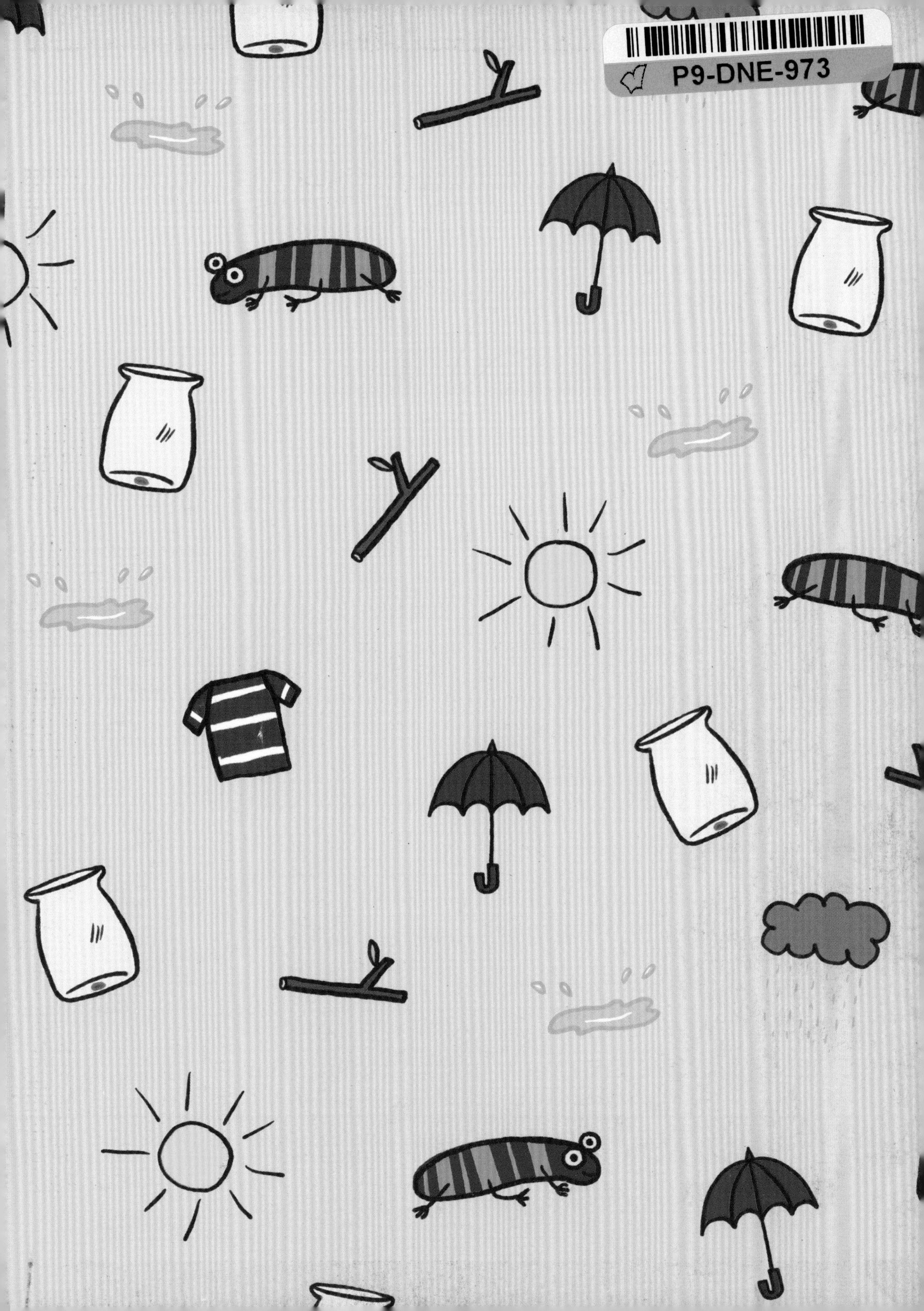

Lucy Harley

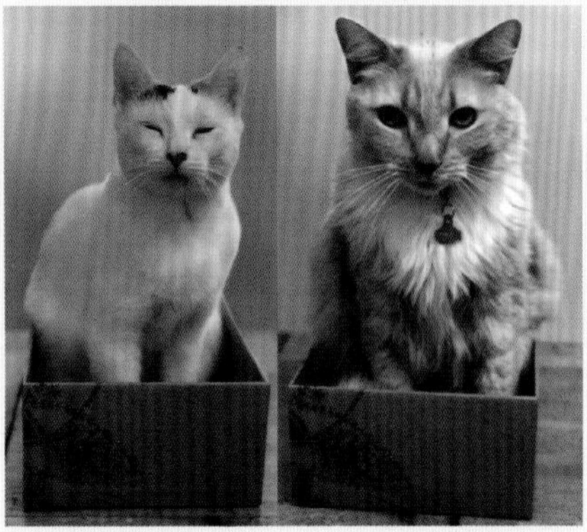

This book is dedicated to my cats, Lucy and Harley.
They were my inspiration for the Cat in this book.
Harley has the outside look and Lucy has the personality.
And they both really like boxes!

About This Book

The text was set in Colby; hand-lettering by Charise Mericle Harper.

This book is a work of fiction. Names, characters, places, and incidents are the product of the author's imagination or are used fictitiously. Any resemblance to actual events, locales, or persons, living or dead, is coincidental. Copyright © 2021 by Charise Mericle Harper · Cover illustration copyright © 2021 by Charise Mericle Harper. Cover copyright © 2021 by Hachette Book Group, Inc. · Hachette Book Group supports the right to free expression and the value of copyright. The purpose of copyright is to encourage writers and artists to produce the creative works that enrich our culture. · The scanning, uploading, and distribution of this book without permission is a theft of the author's intellectual property. If you would like permission to use material from the book (other than for review purposes), please contact permissions@hbgusa.com. Thank you for your support of the author's rights. · Little, Brown and Company · Hachette Book Group · 1290 Avenue of the Americas, New York, NY 10104 · Visit us at LBYR.com · First Edition: September 2021 · Little, Brown and Company is a division of Hachette Book Group, Inc. · The Little, Brown name and logo are trademarks of Hachette Book Group, Inc. · The publisher is not responsible for websites (or their content) that are not owned by the publisher. · Library of Congress Cataloging-in-Publication Data · Names: Harper, Charise Mericle, author, illustrator. · Title: Pepper & Boo: puddle trouble / by Charise Mericle Harper. · Other titles: Pepper and Boo: puddle trouble · Description: First edition. | New York : Little, Brown and Company, 2021. | Audience: Ages 6-10. | Summary: Boo is excited about playing in the rain, while Pepper would rather stay indoors with the Cat until Boo finds a warm coat for Pepper—or the rain stops. · Identifiers: LCCN 2020054847 | ISBN 9780759555082 · Subjects: CYAC: Dogs—Fiction. | Cats—Fiction. | Rain and rainfall—Fiction. | Humorous stories. Classification: LCC PZ7.H231323 Pep 2021 | DDC [E]—dc23 · LC record available at https://lccn.loc.gov/2020054847 · ISBN 978-0-7595-5508-2 · PRINTED IN CHINA · APS · 10 9 8 7 6 5 4 3

PEPPER & BOO

PUDDLE TROUBLE

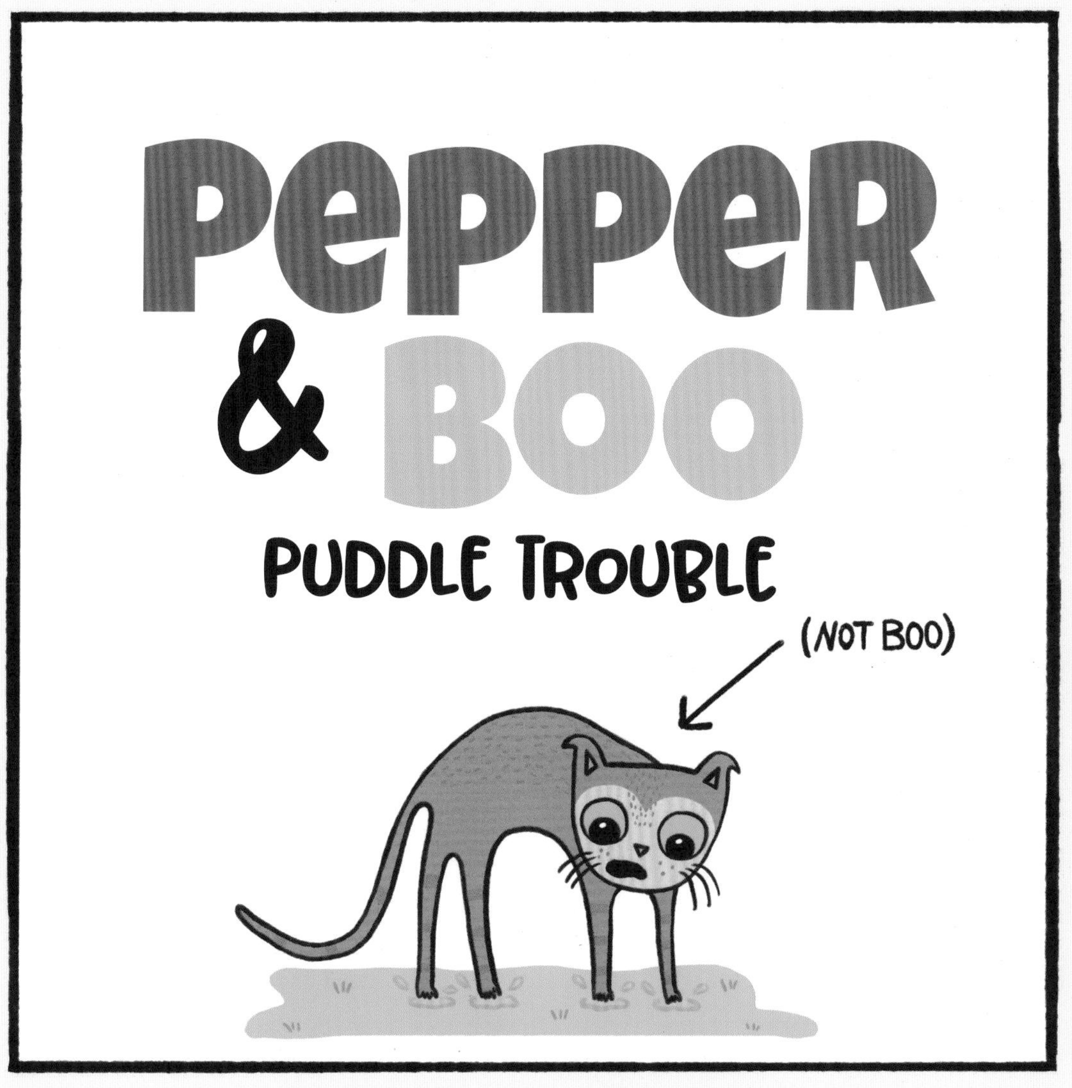
(NOT BOO)

by Charise Mericle Harper

LB
Little, Brown and Company
New York Boston

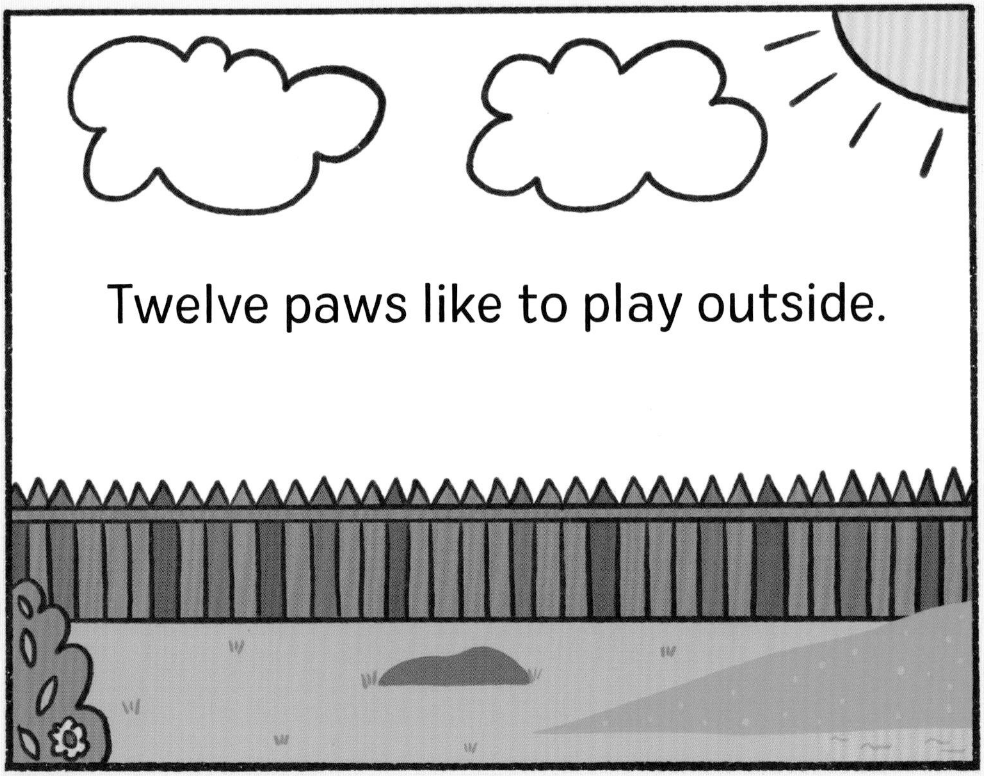
Twelve paws like to play outside.

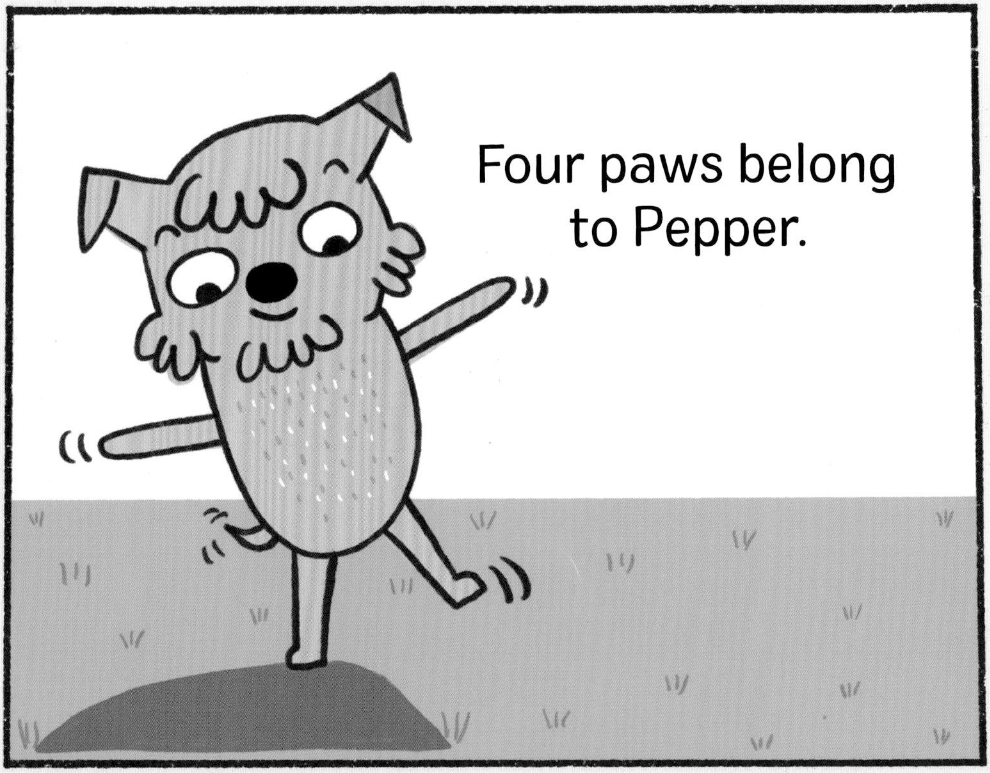
Four paws belong to Pepper.

Four paws belong to Boo.

Four paws belong to the Cat.
The Cat has a message.

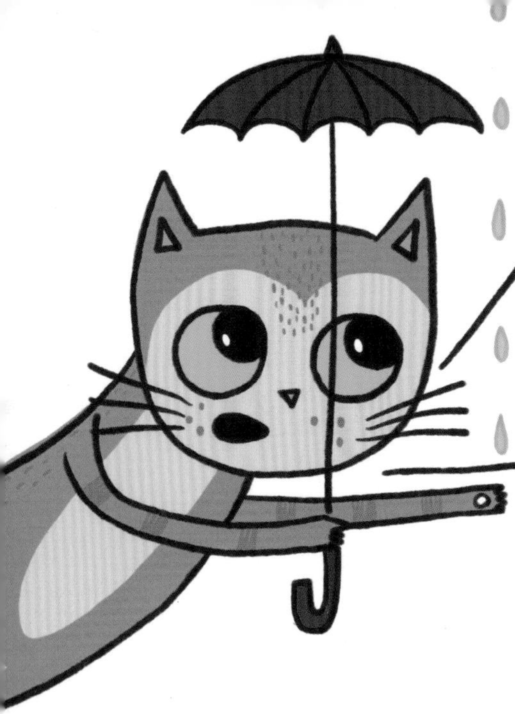

I like to play outside.

BUT...

it is raining.

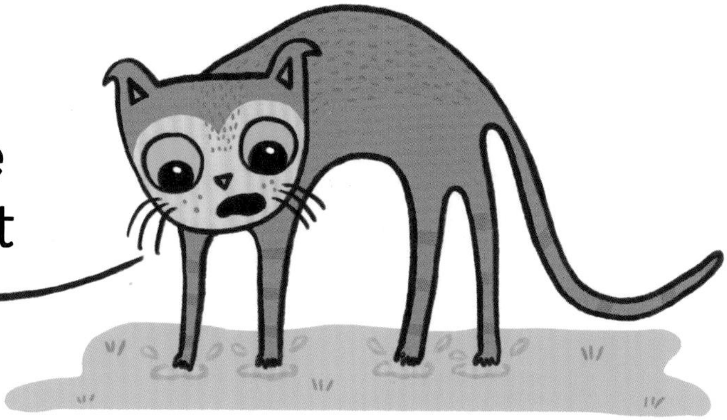

I do not like
squishy, wet
paws.

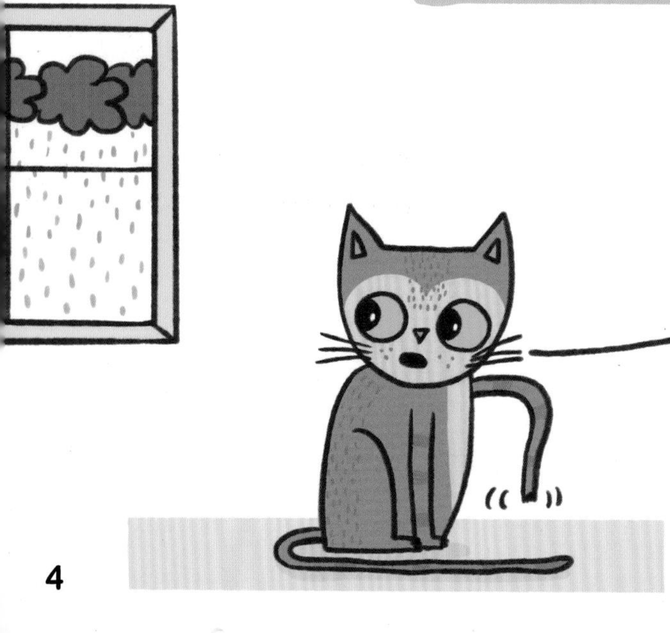

I am a cat.
I will stay inside.

A cat can have fun inside.

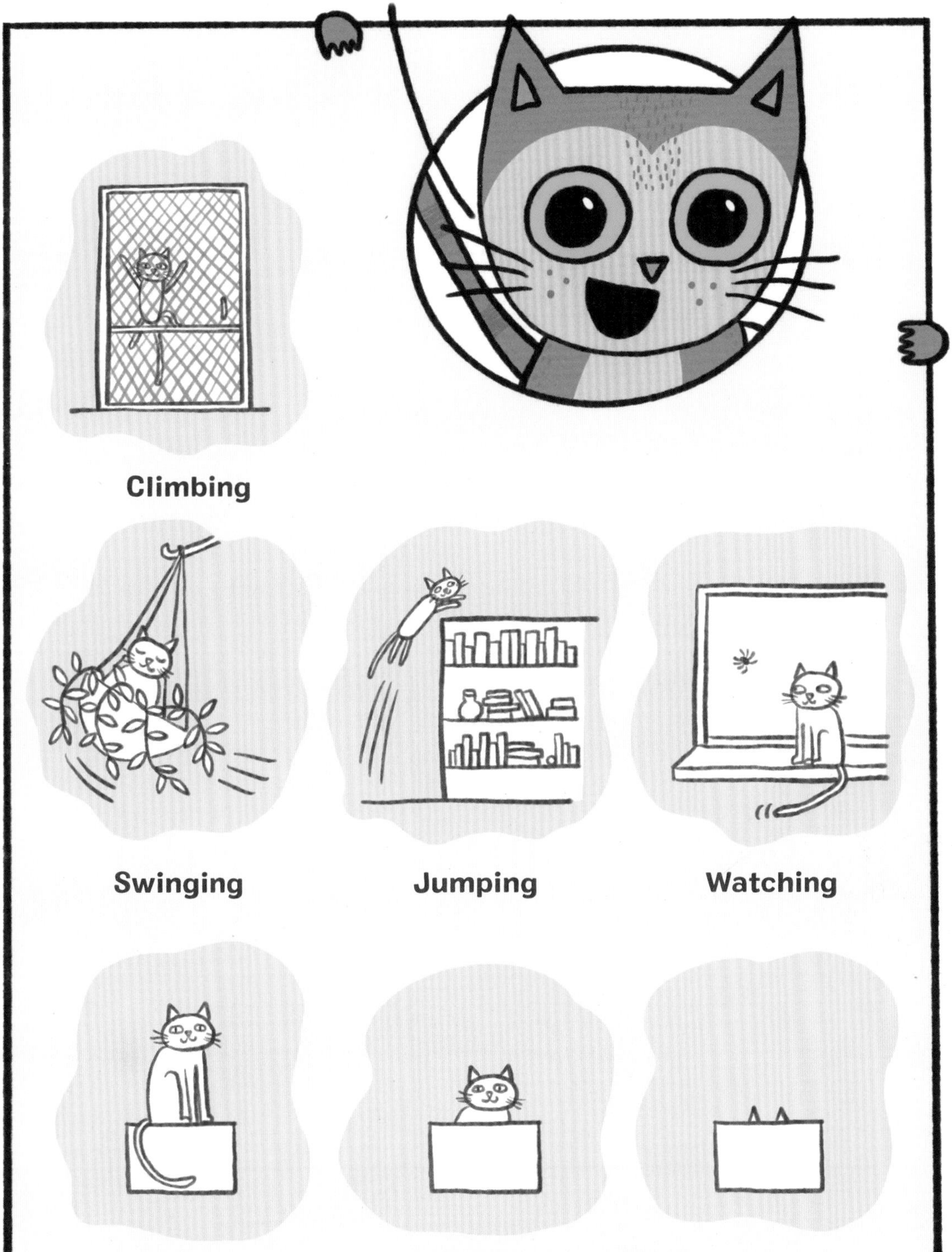

Climbing
Swinging
Jumping
Watching
Sitting on
Sitting in
Hiding

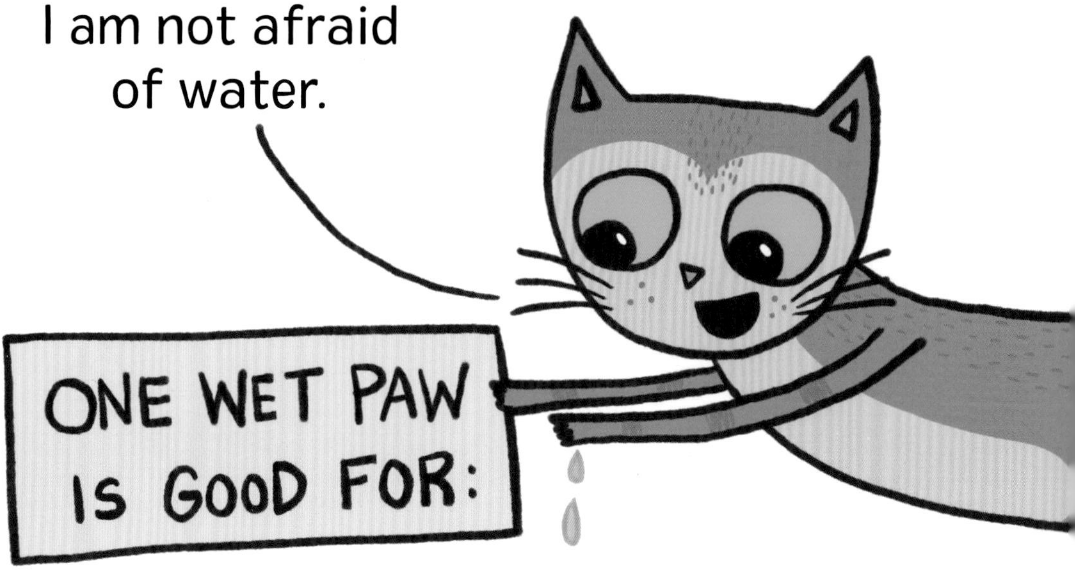
I am not afraid of water.
ONE WET PAW IS GOOD FOR:

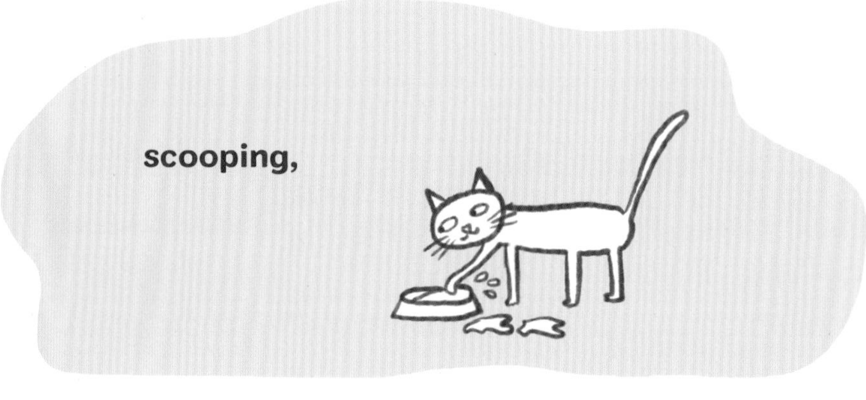
scooping,

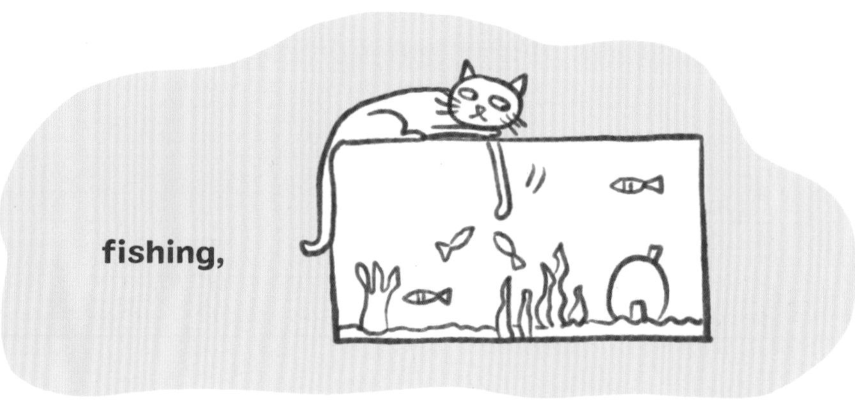
fishing,

drinking,

1: dip   2: lick

exploring,

and playing.

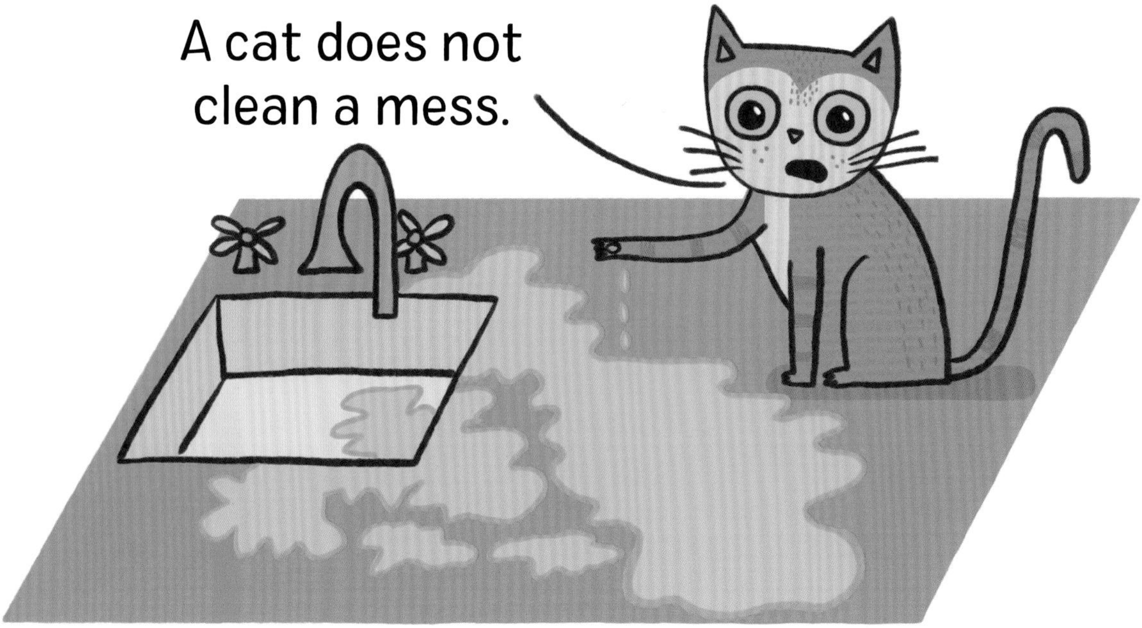
A cat does not
clean a mess.

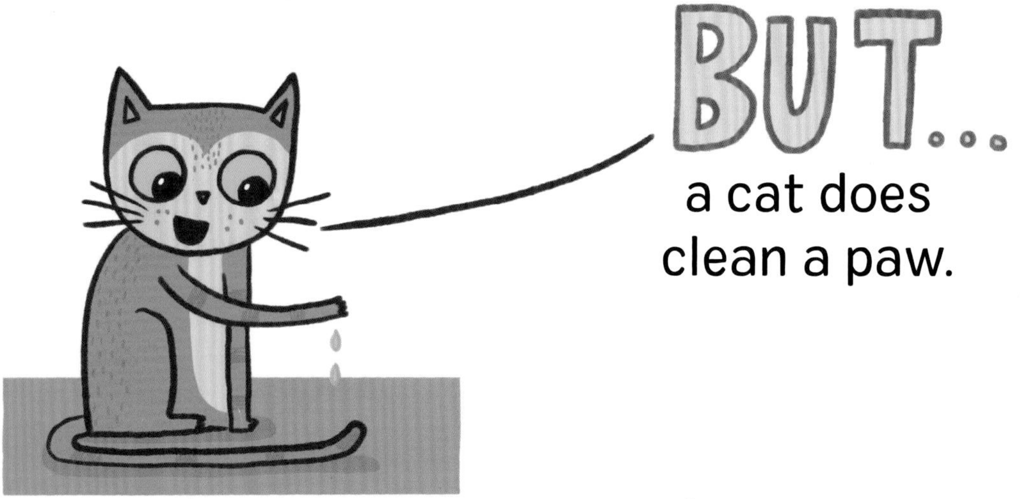
BUT...
a cat does
clean a paw.

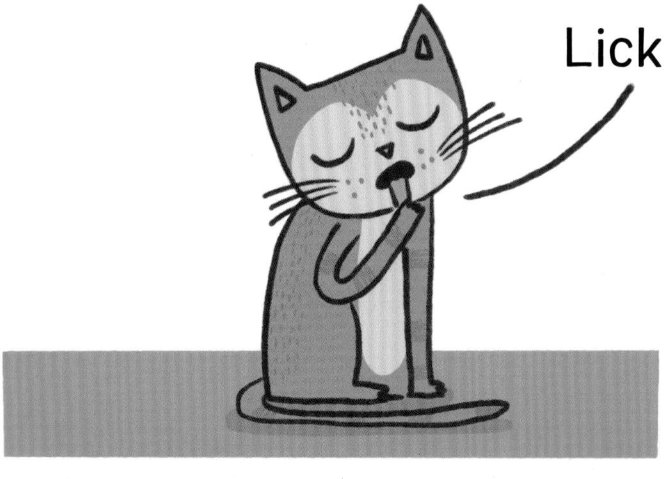
Lick.

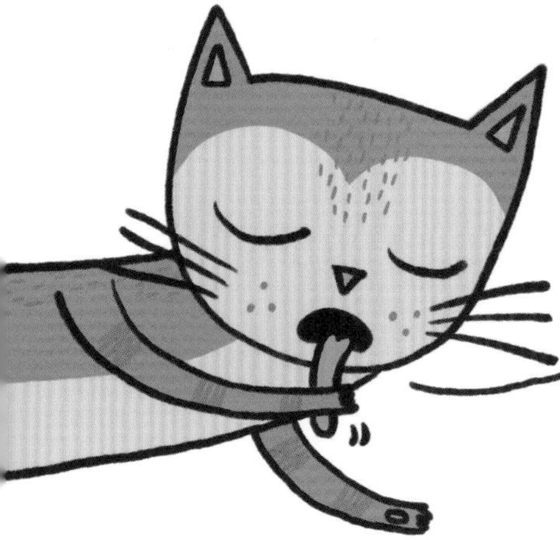

Lick.

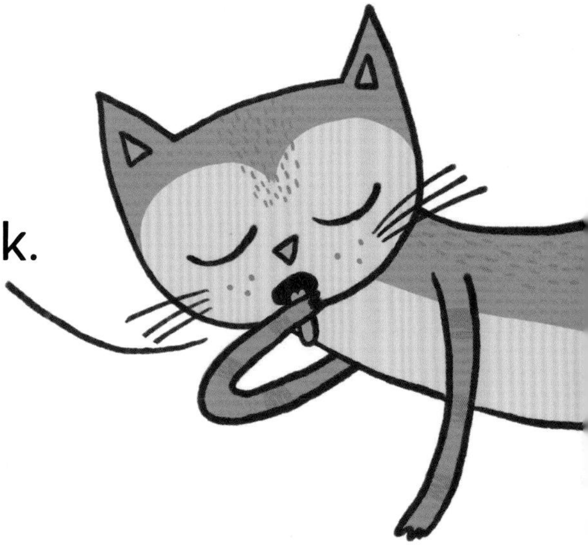

Lick.

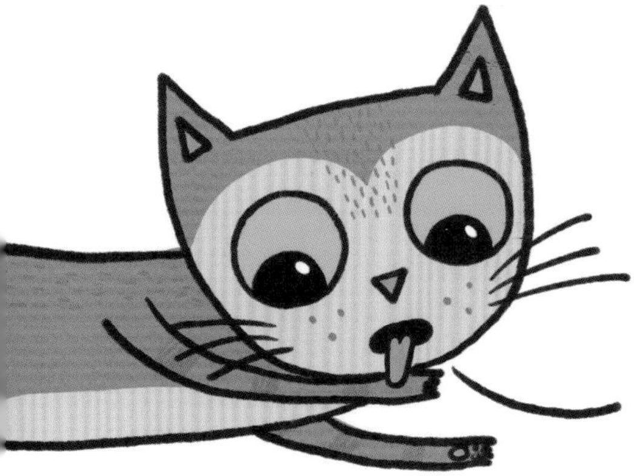

Lick.

Done!
Four little
toe beans as
cute as new.

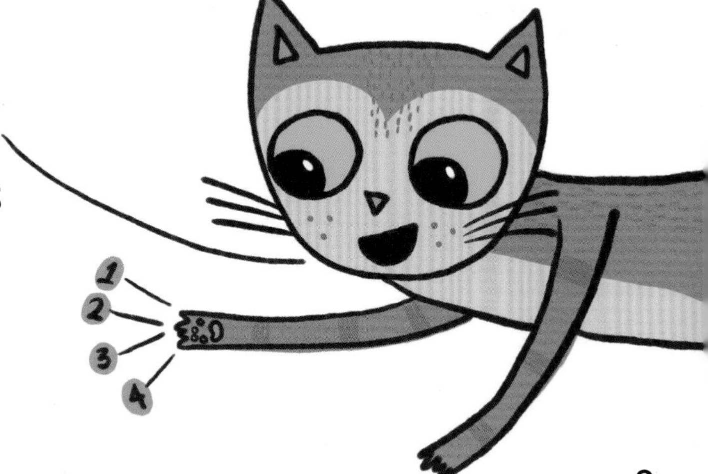
1
2
3
4

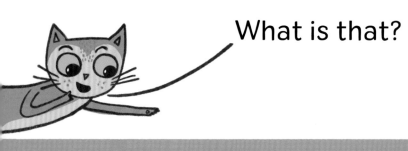

What is that?

A jar...
with A TREAT?

A yummy treat!
It will be mine.

WIGGLE

WIGGLE

JIGGLE

JIGGLE

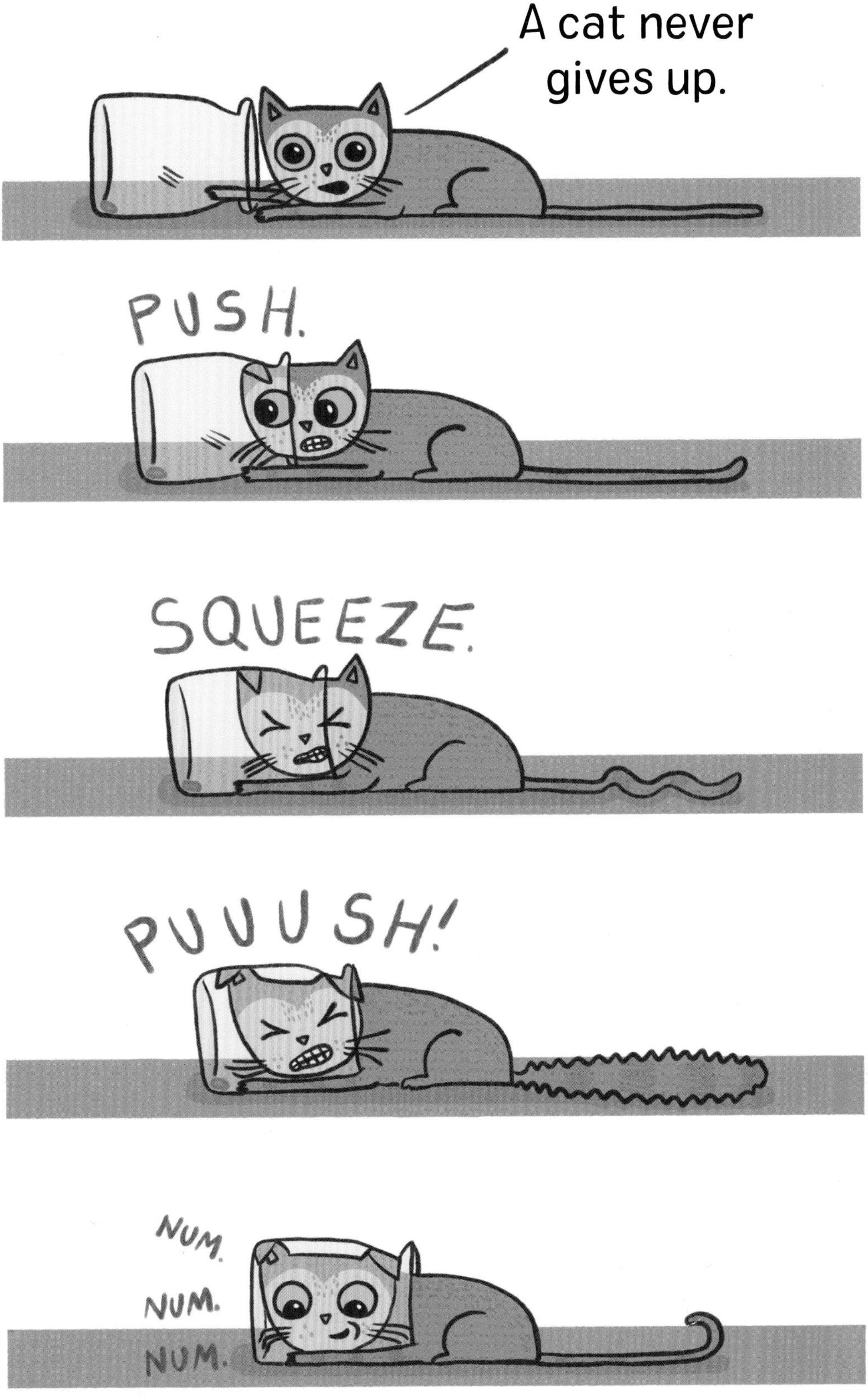
A cat never gives up.
PUSH.
SQUEEZE.
PUUUSH!
NUM.
NUM.
NUM.

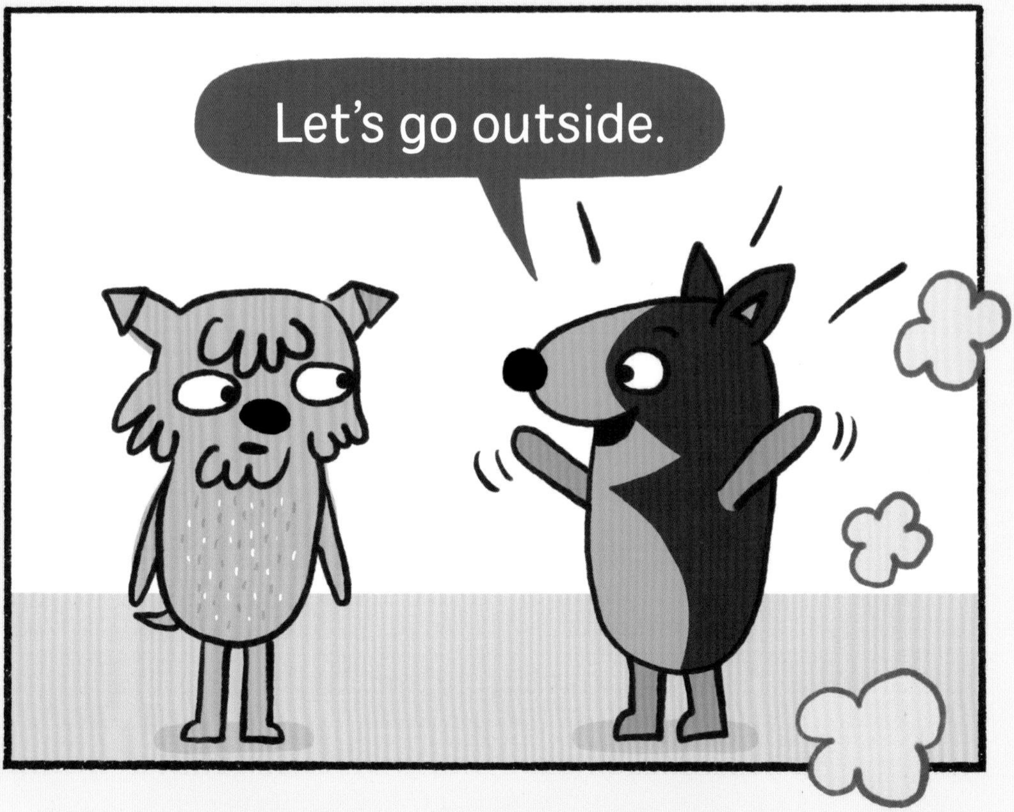
Let's go outside.

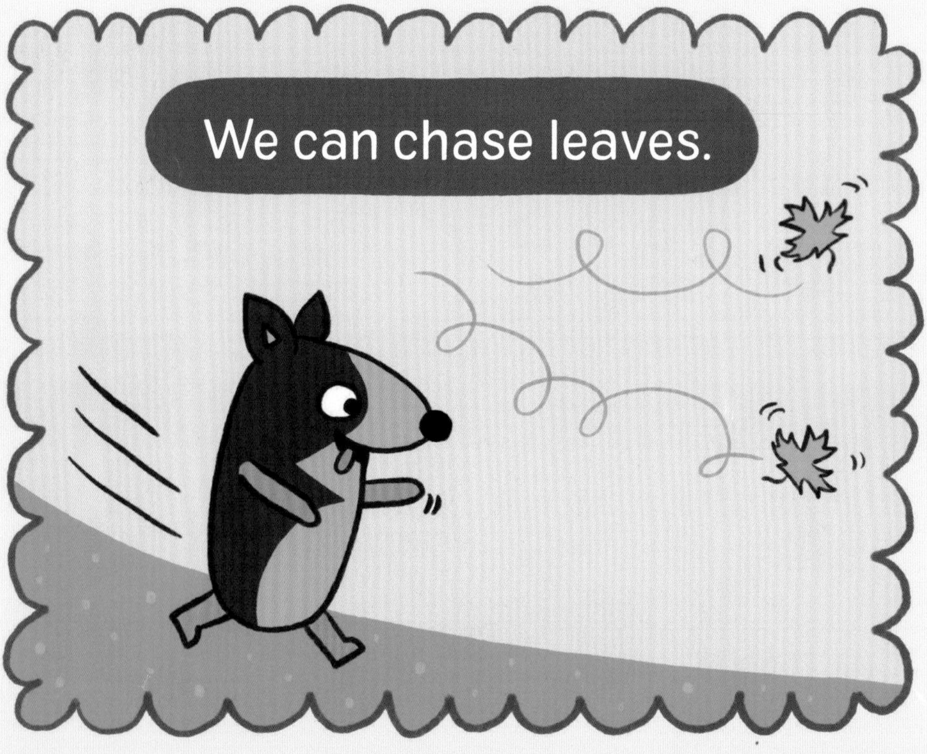
We can chase leaves.

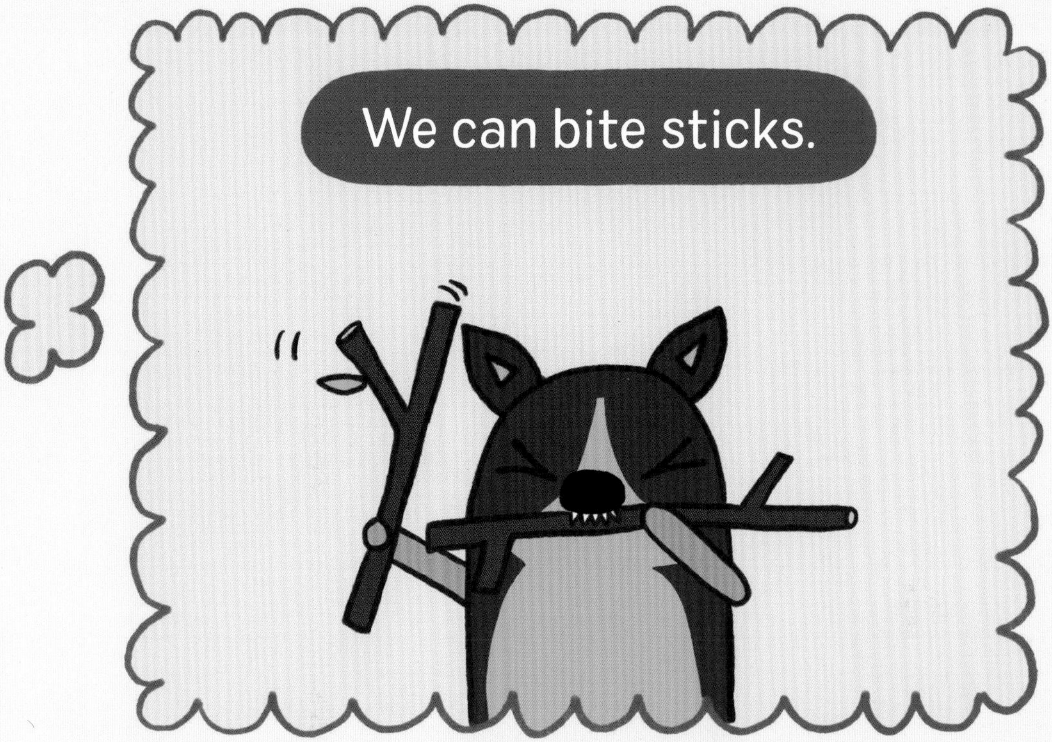
We can bite sticks.

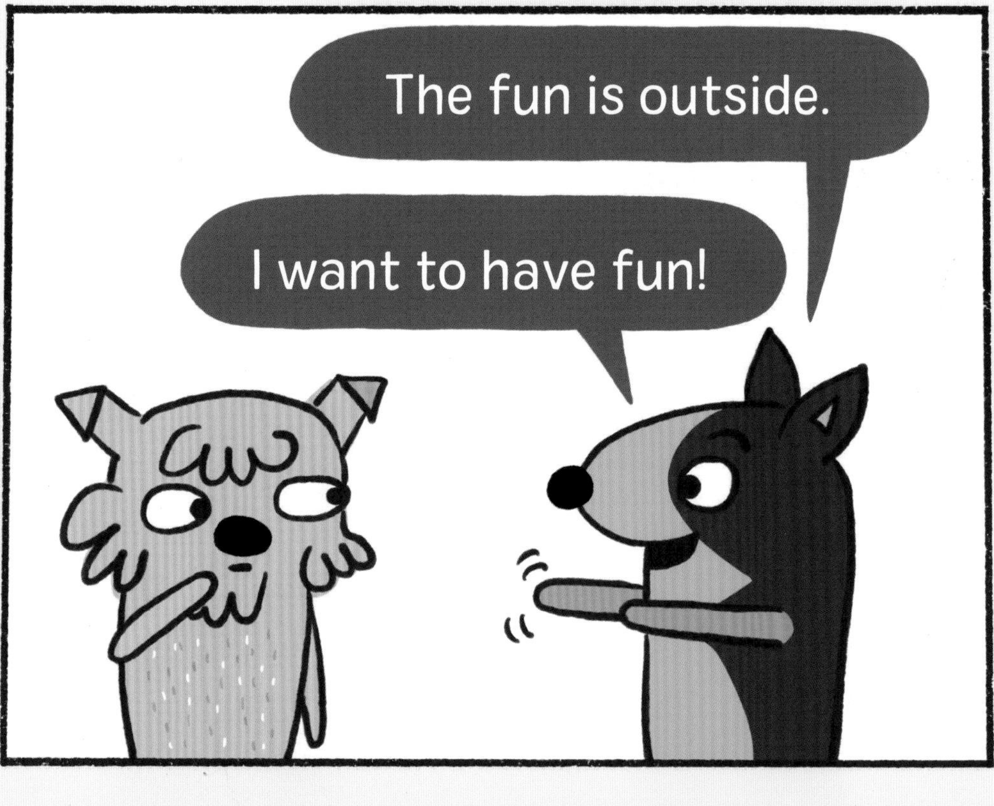
The fun is outside.
I want to have fun!

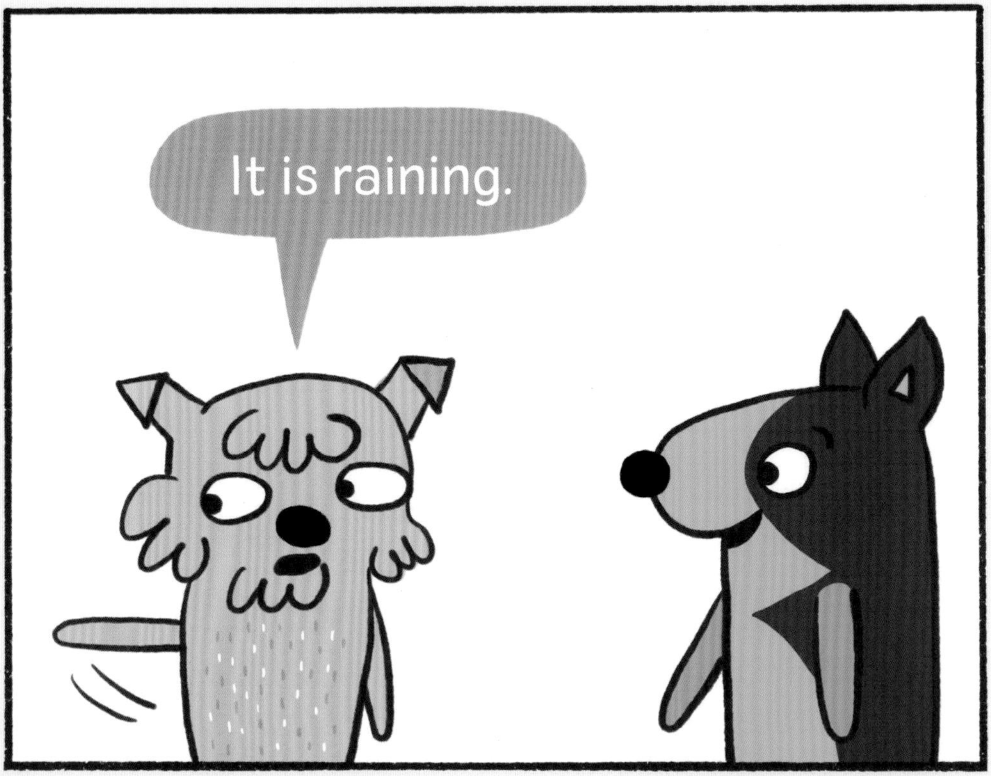
It is raining.

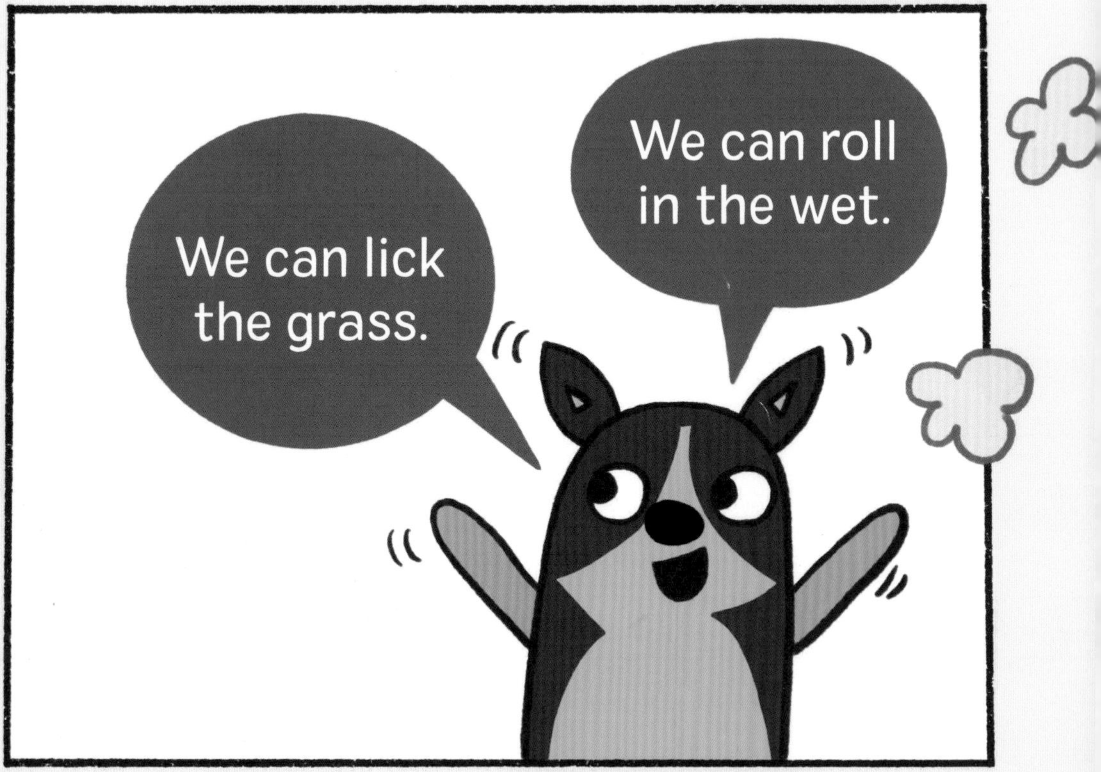
We can lick the grass.
We can roll in the wet.

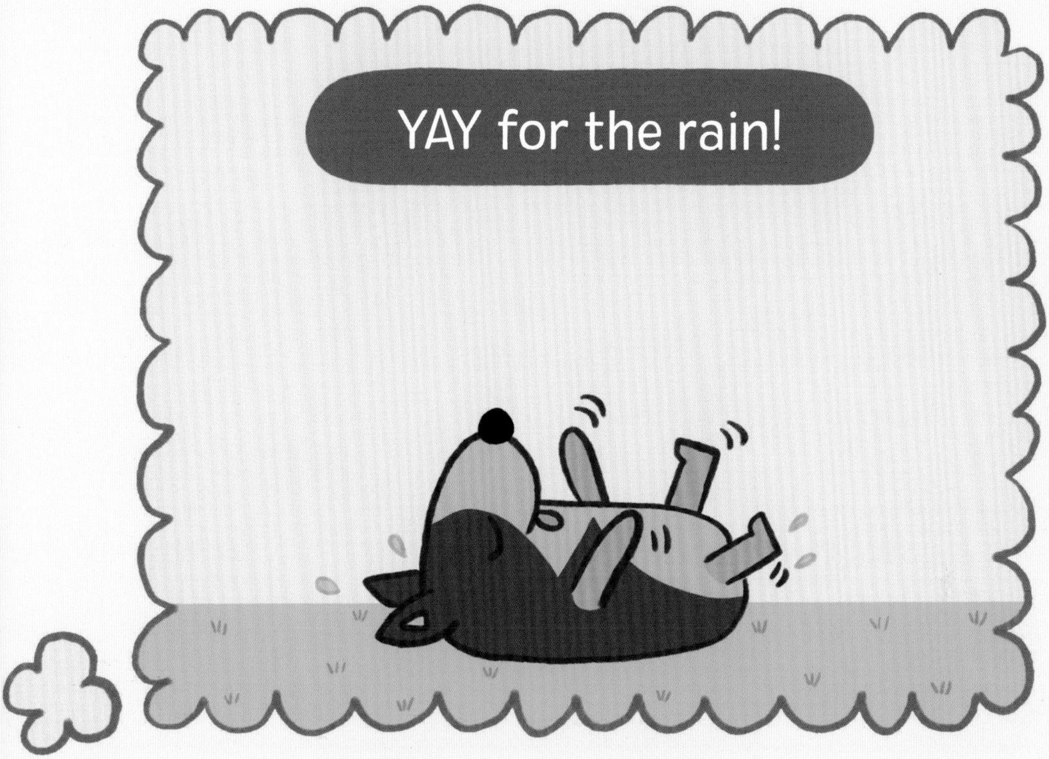
YAY for the rain!

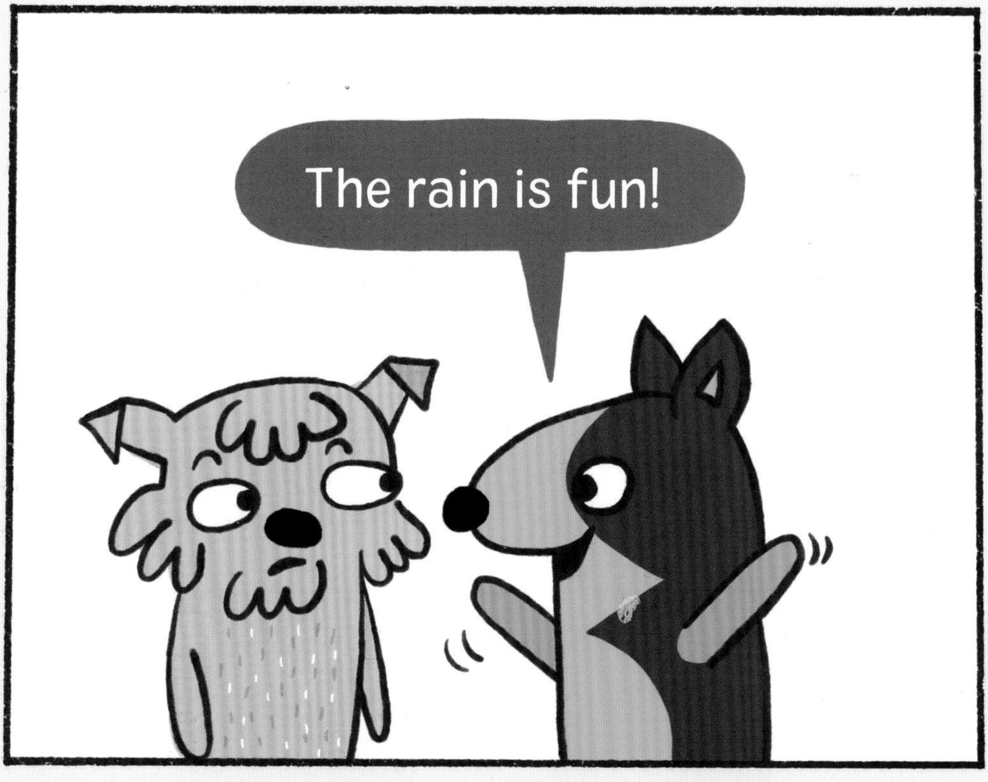
The rain is fun!

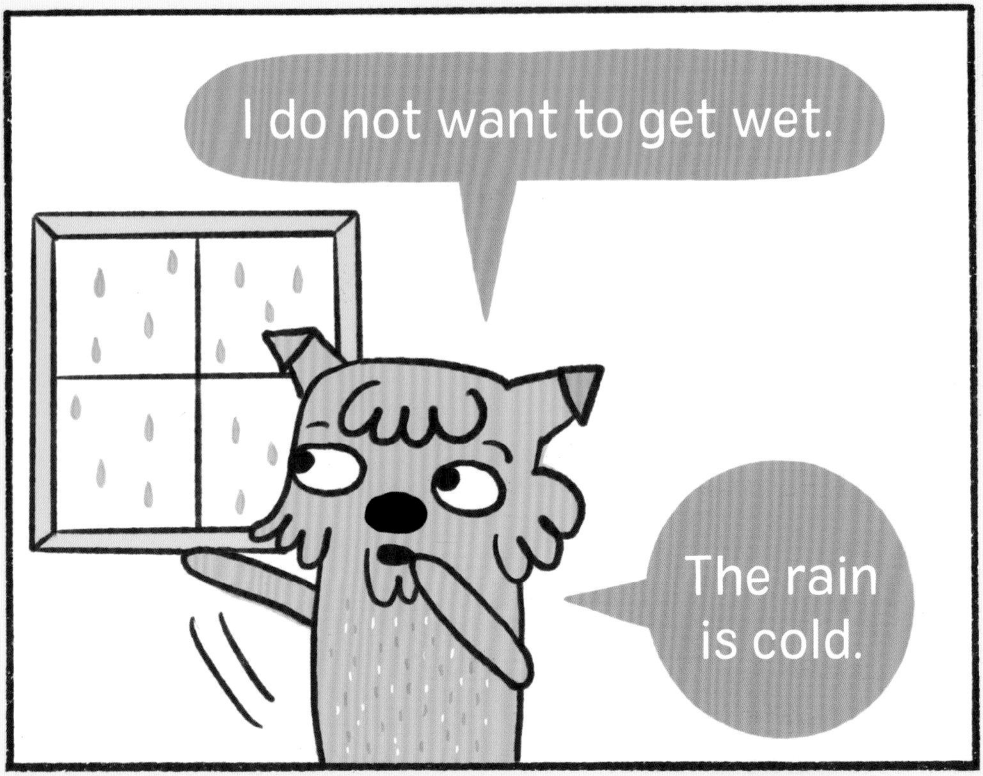
I do not want to get wet.
The rain is cold.

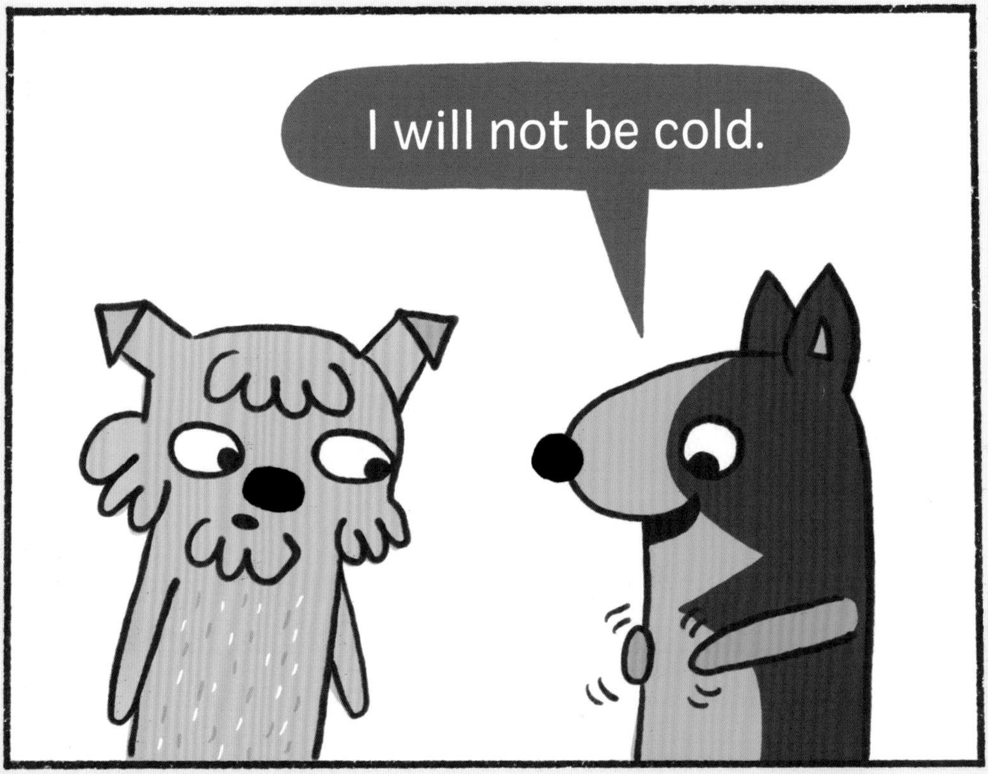
I will not be cold.

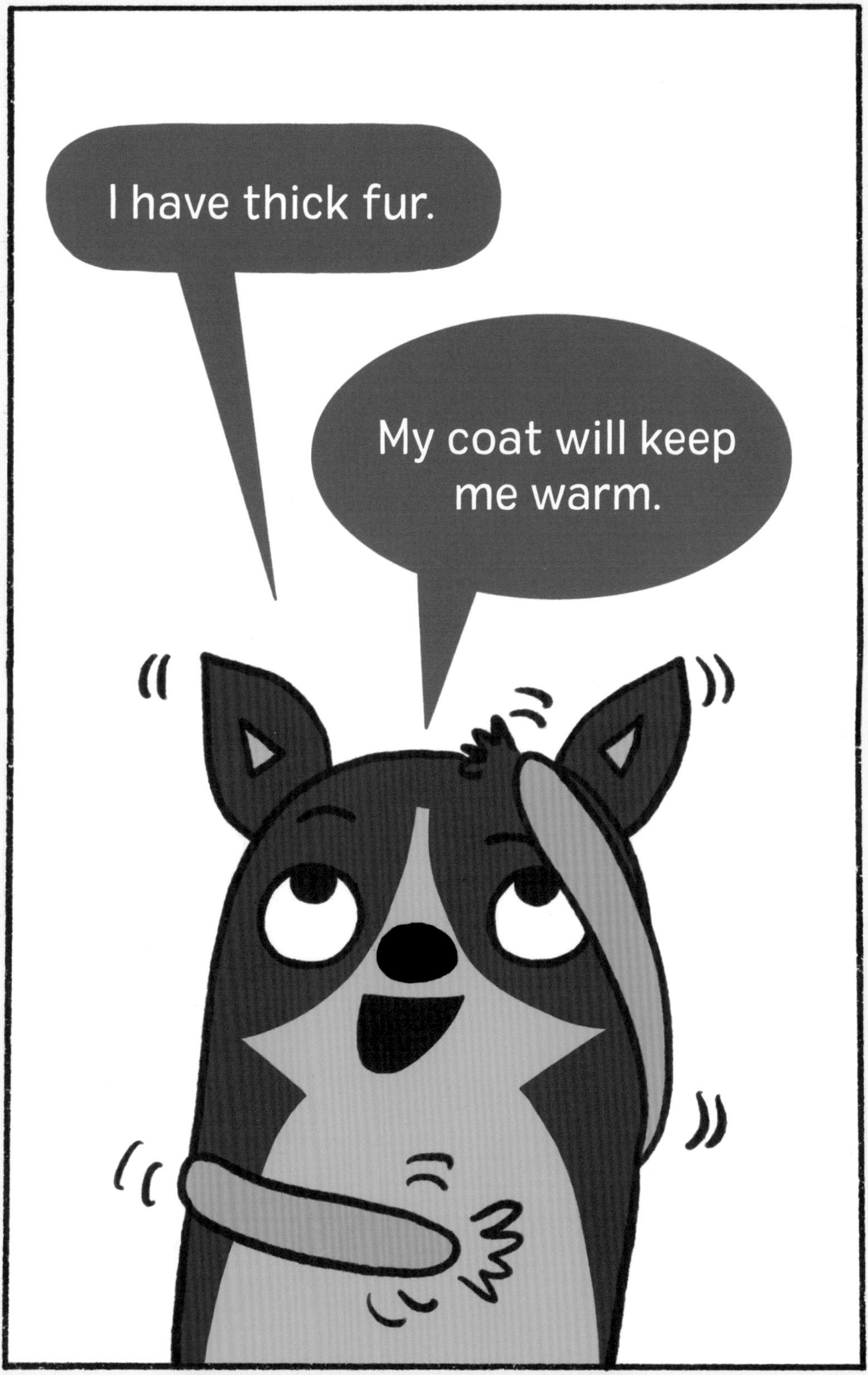
I have thick fur.
My coat will keep me warm.

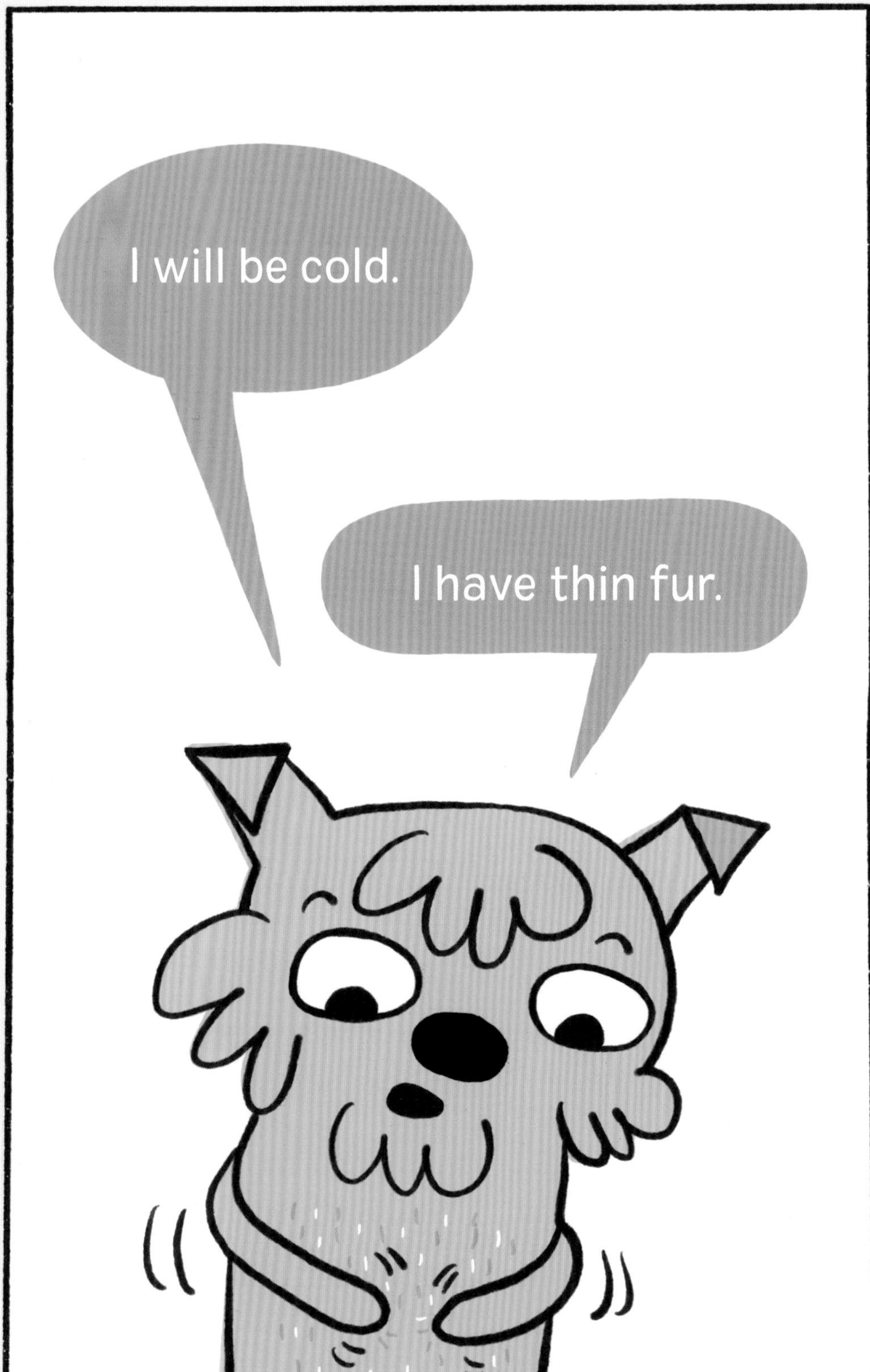
I will be cold.
I have thin fur.

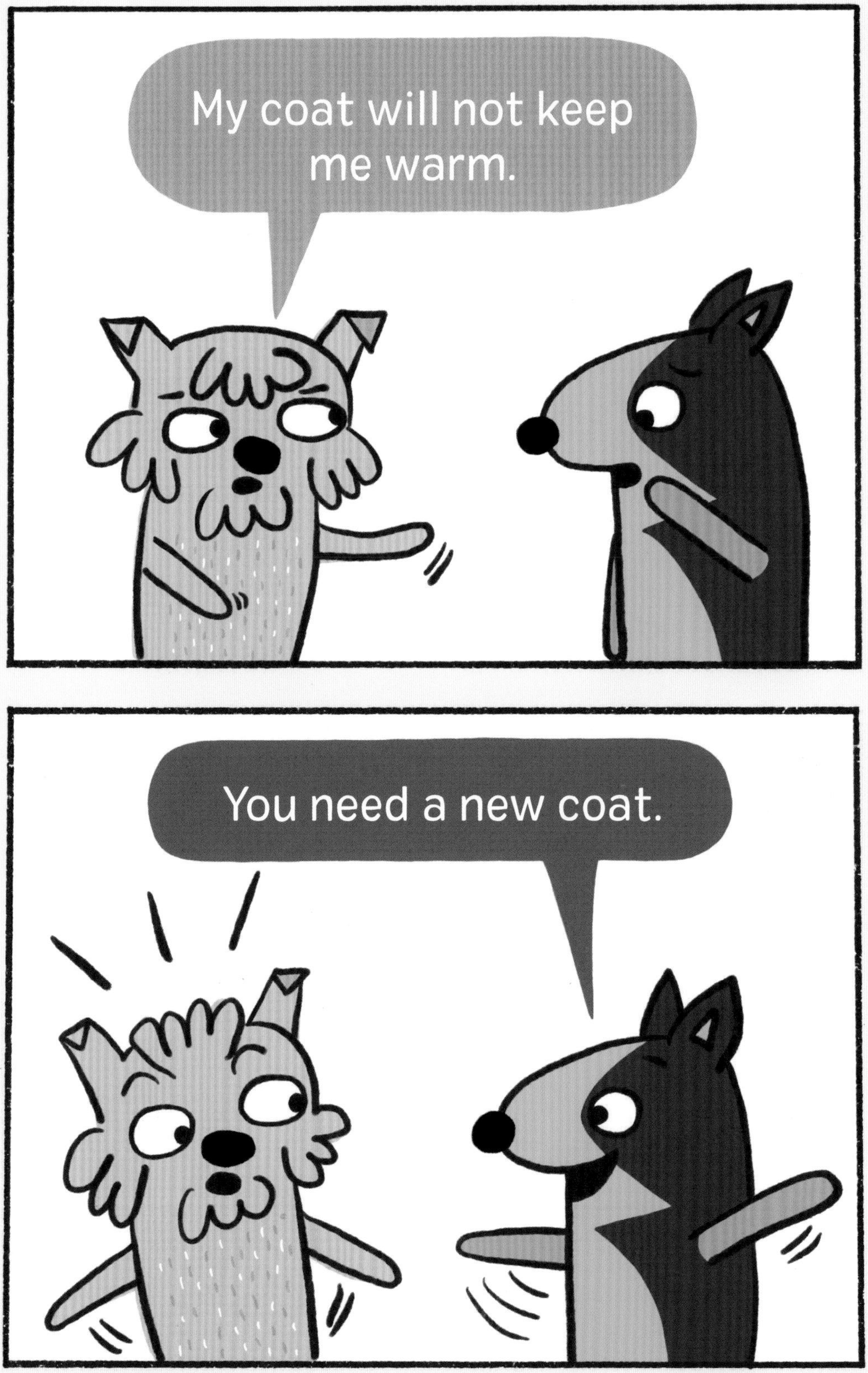
My coat will not keep me warm.
You need a new coat.

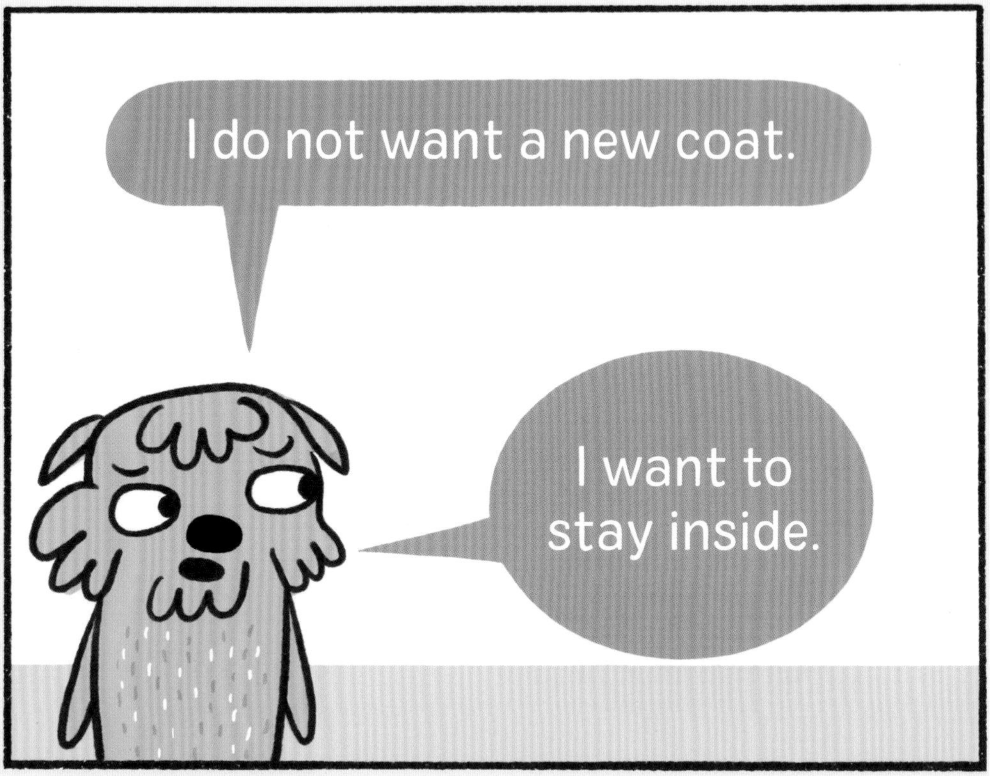
I do not want a new coat.
I want to stay inside.

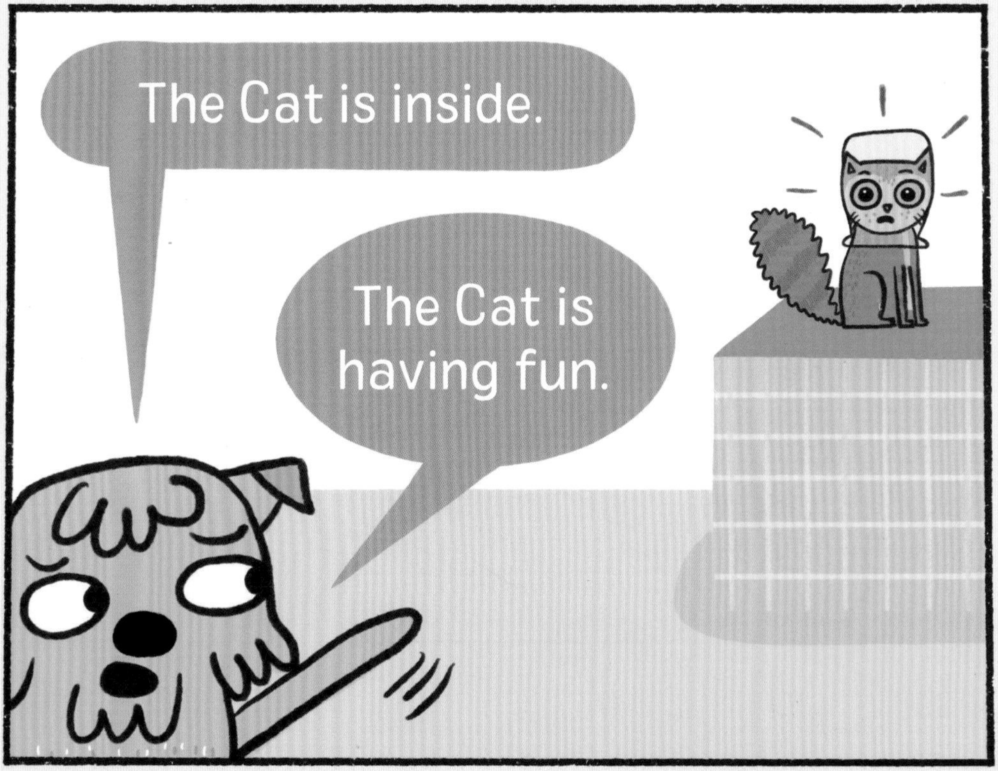
The Cat is inside.
The Cat is having fun.

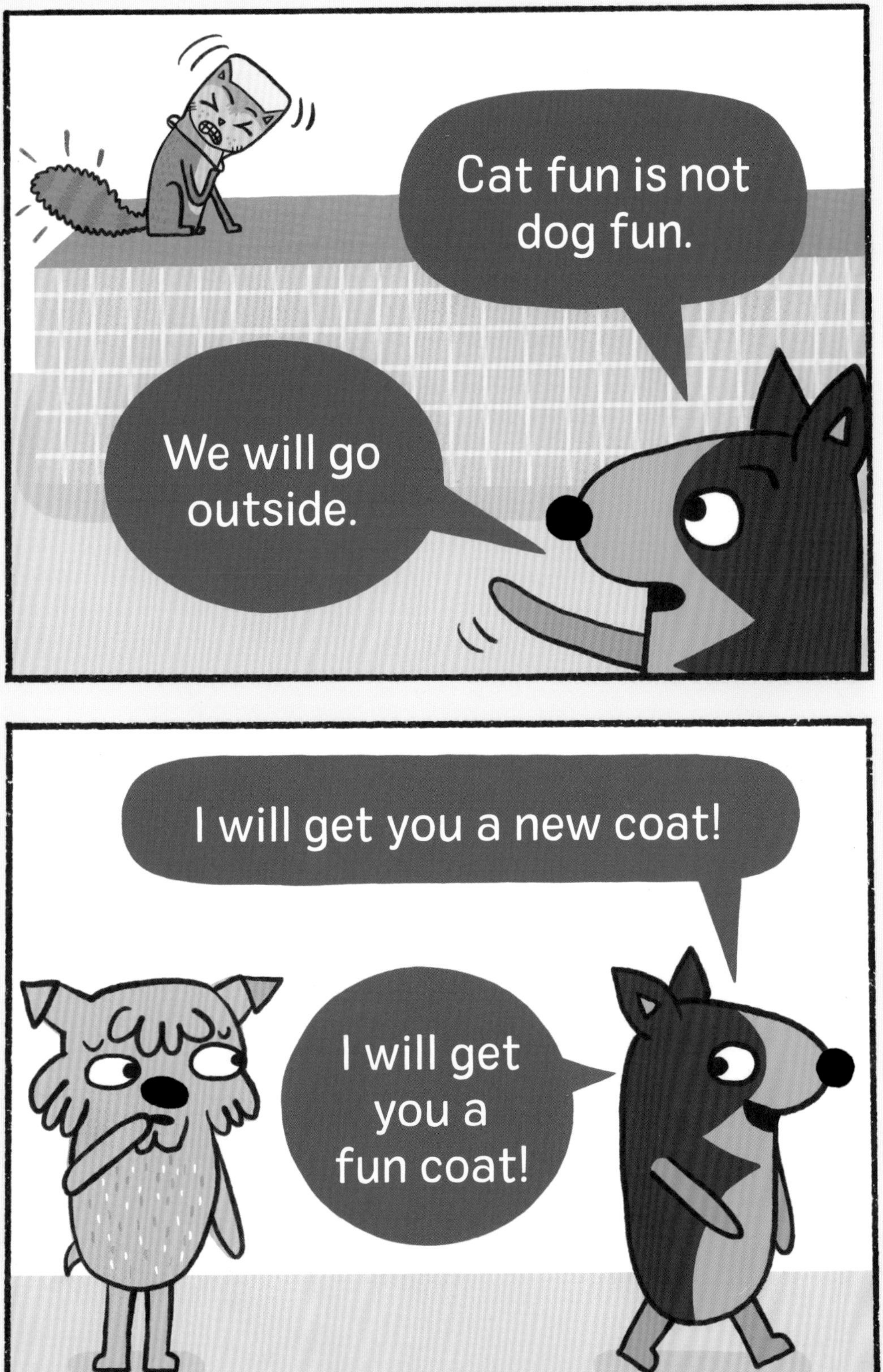
Cat fun is not dog fun.
We will go outside.
I will get you a new coat!
I will get you a fun coat!

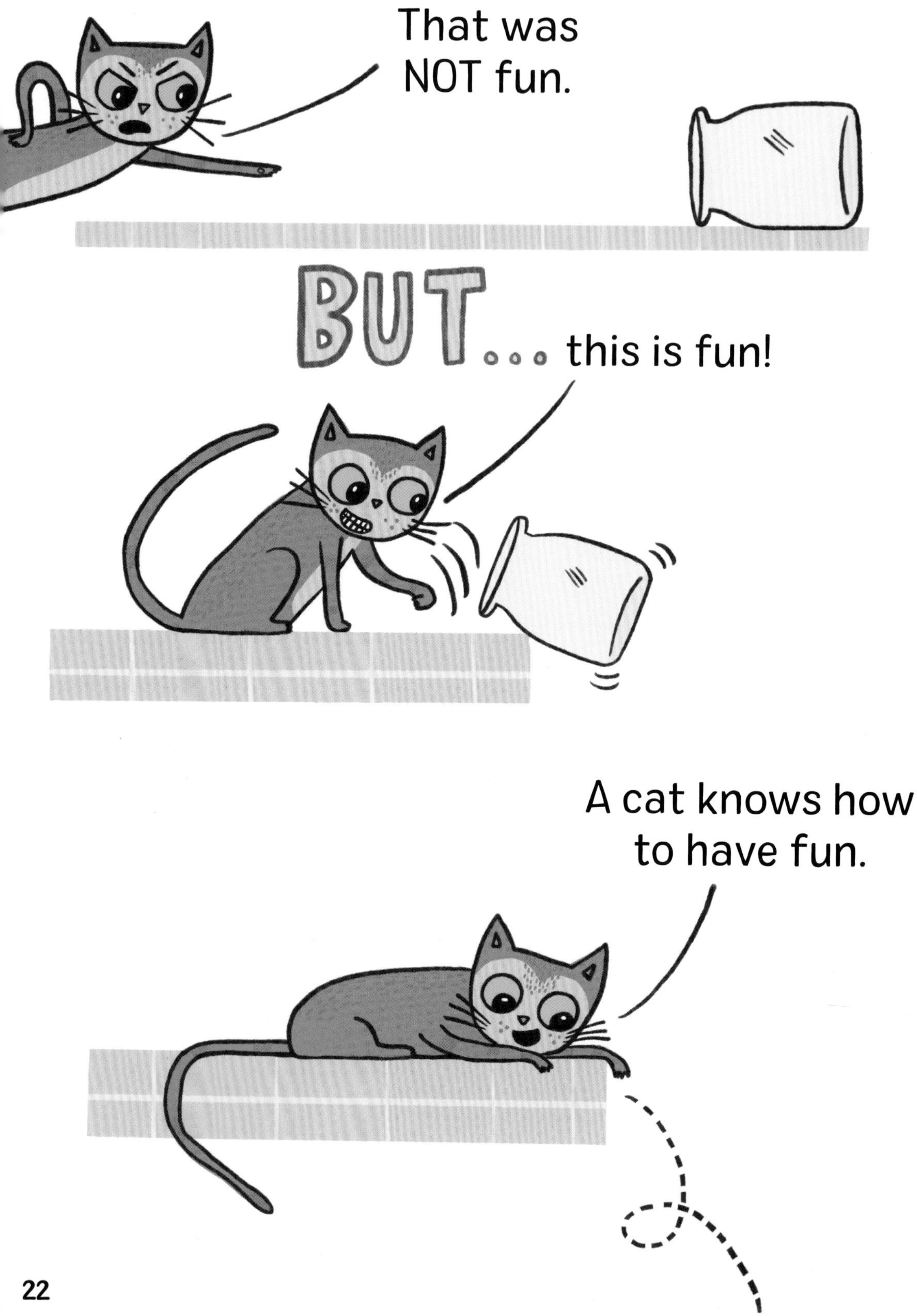
That was NOT fun.
BUT... this is fun!
A cat knows how to have fun.

A cat can have fun with so many things.

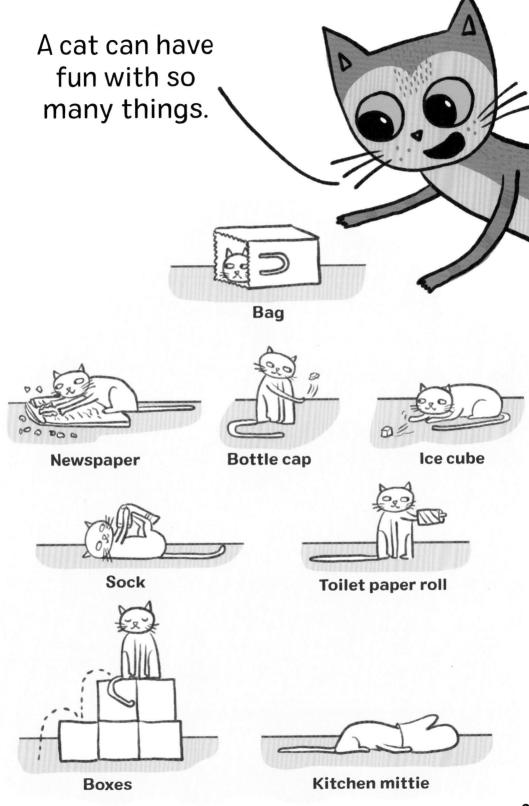

Bag

Newspaper

Bottle cap

Ice cube

Sock

Toilet paper roll

Boxes

Kitchen mittie

23

Sometimes a cat can even have fun with...

Shhhhhh!

This is a secret.
Do not tell anyone.

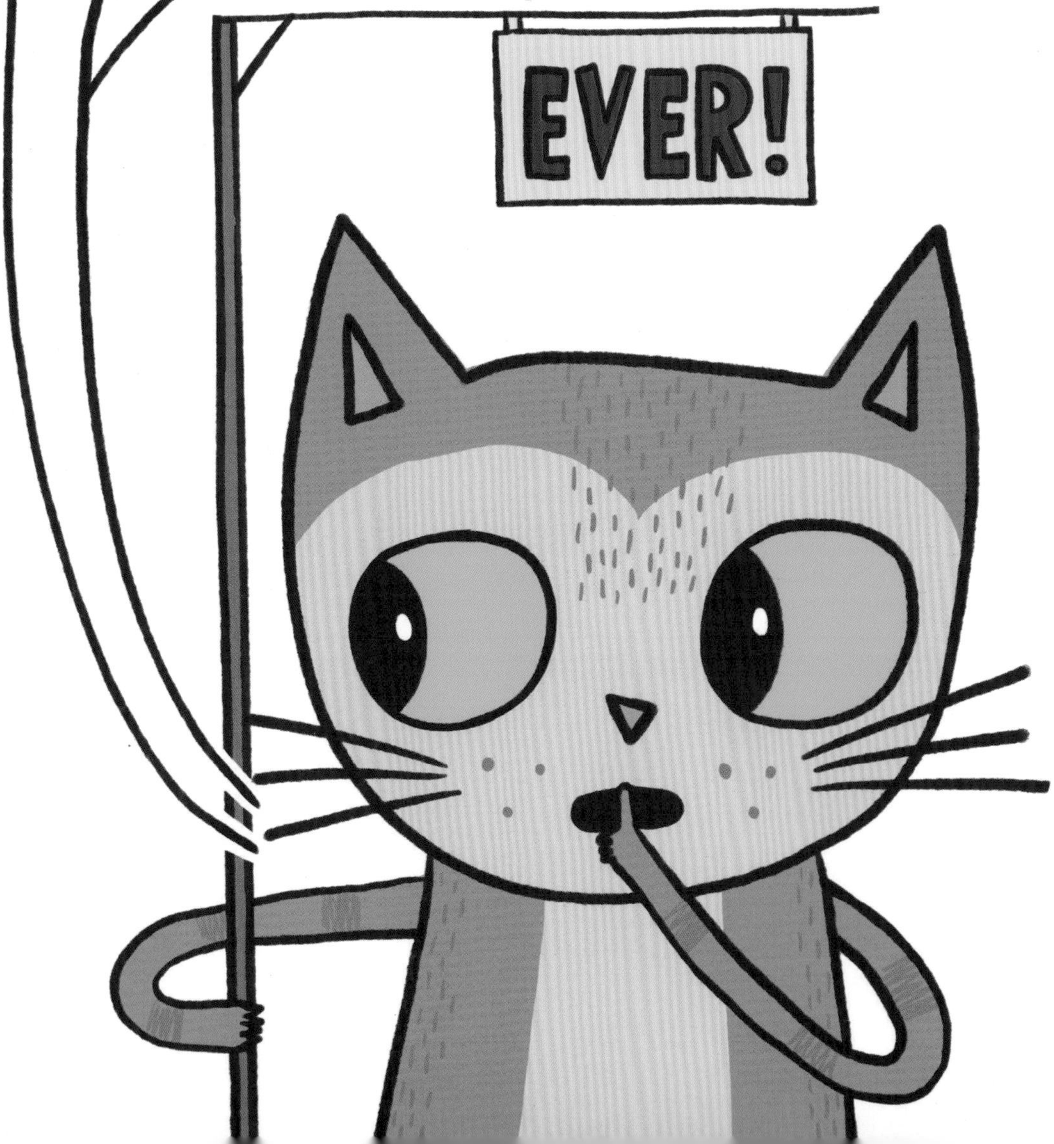
EVER!

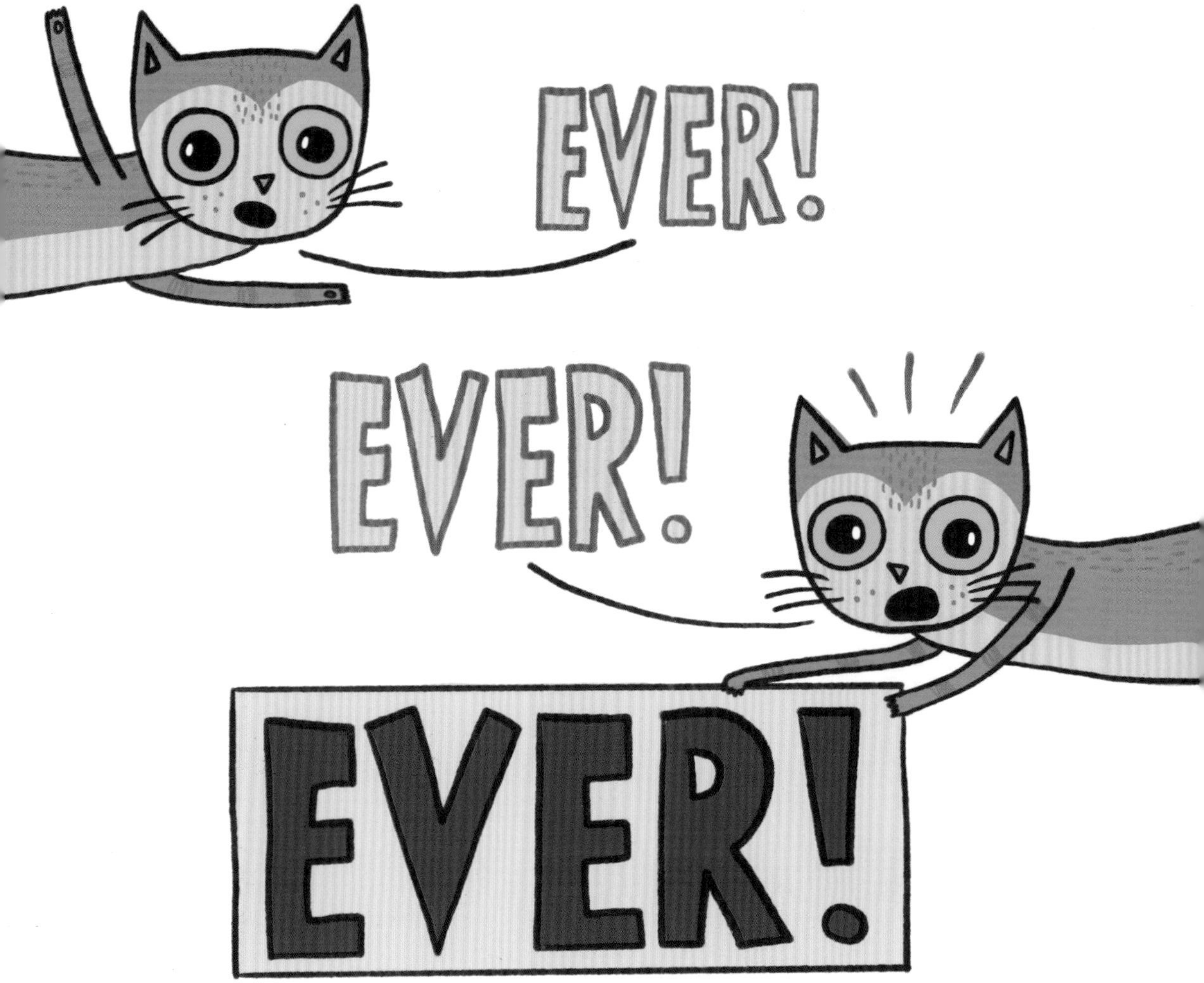
EVER!
EVER!
EVER!

Sometimes a cat can have
fun with a dog toy.

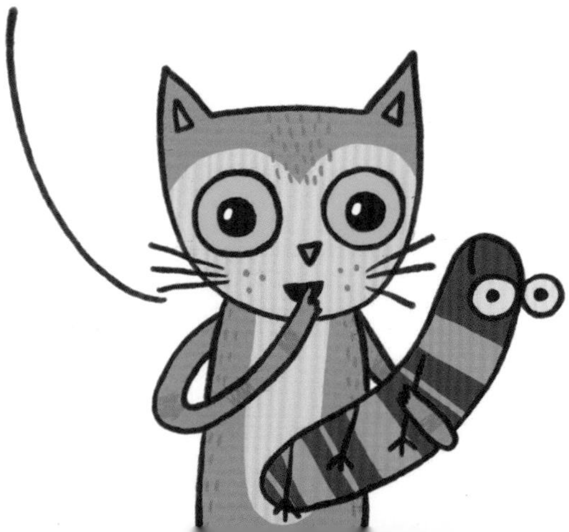

This is a good toy for:

rubbing

and rolling

and pushing

and kicking

and swinging.

BUT...

it is not a good toy for hugging. It has a very loud squeak.

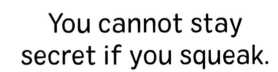

HUG

SQUEAK!

You cannot stay secret if you squeak.

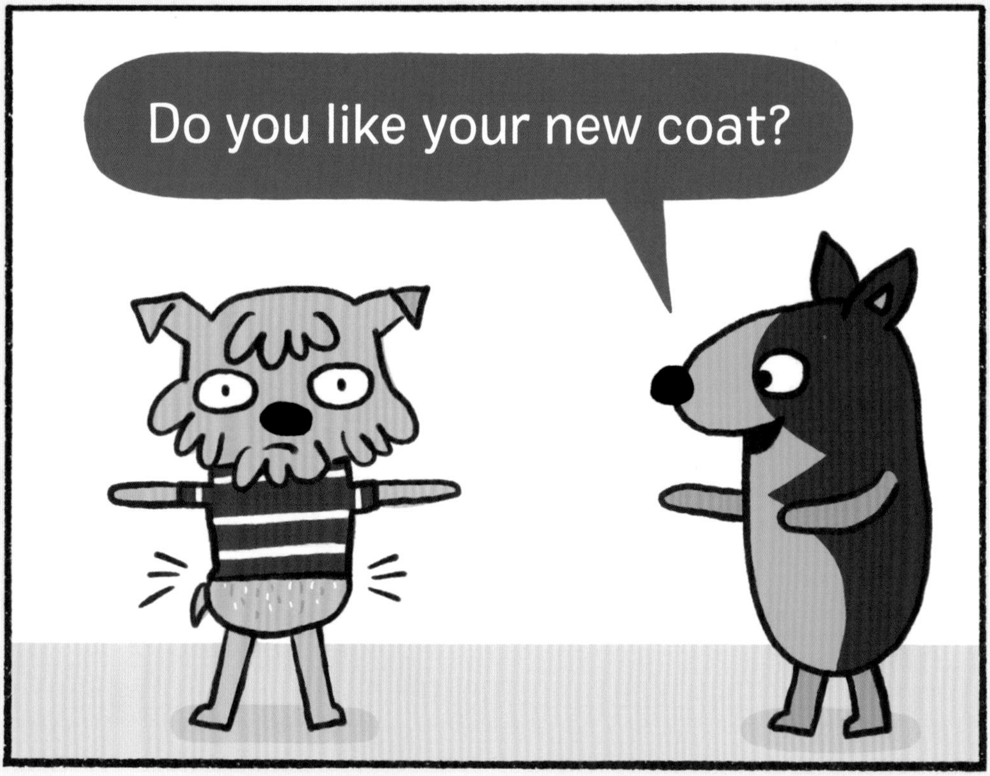
Do you like your new coat?

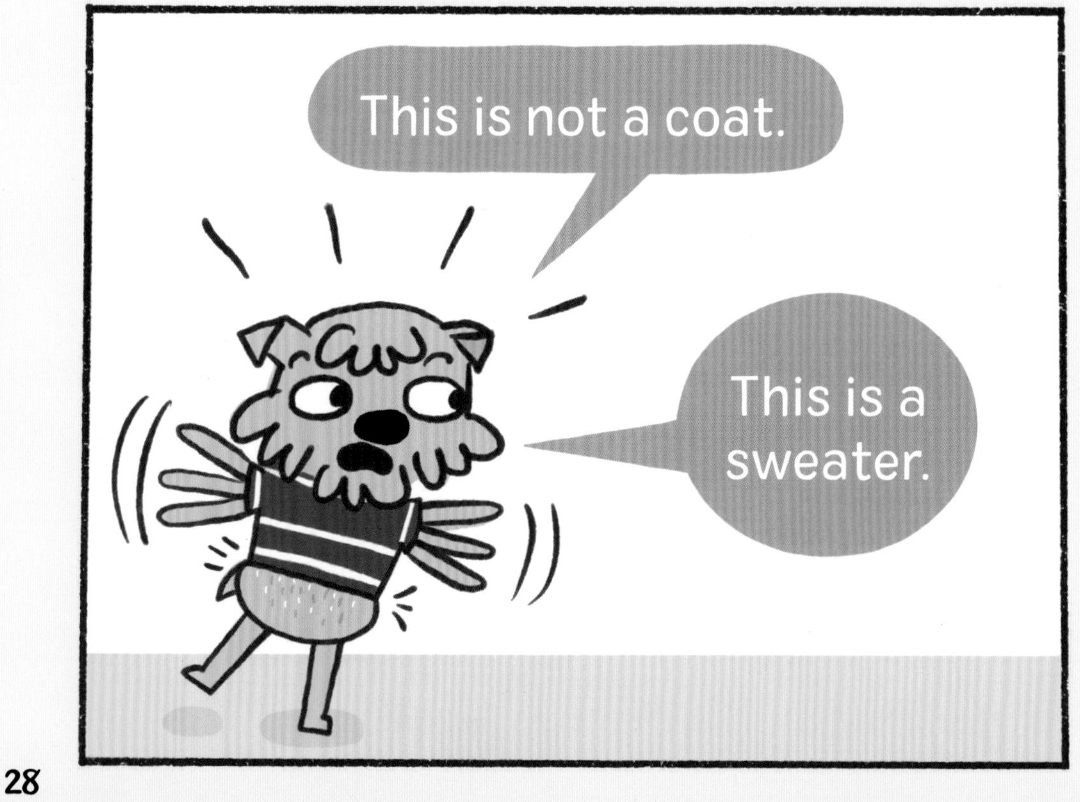
This is not a coat.
This is a sweater.

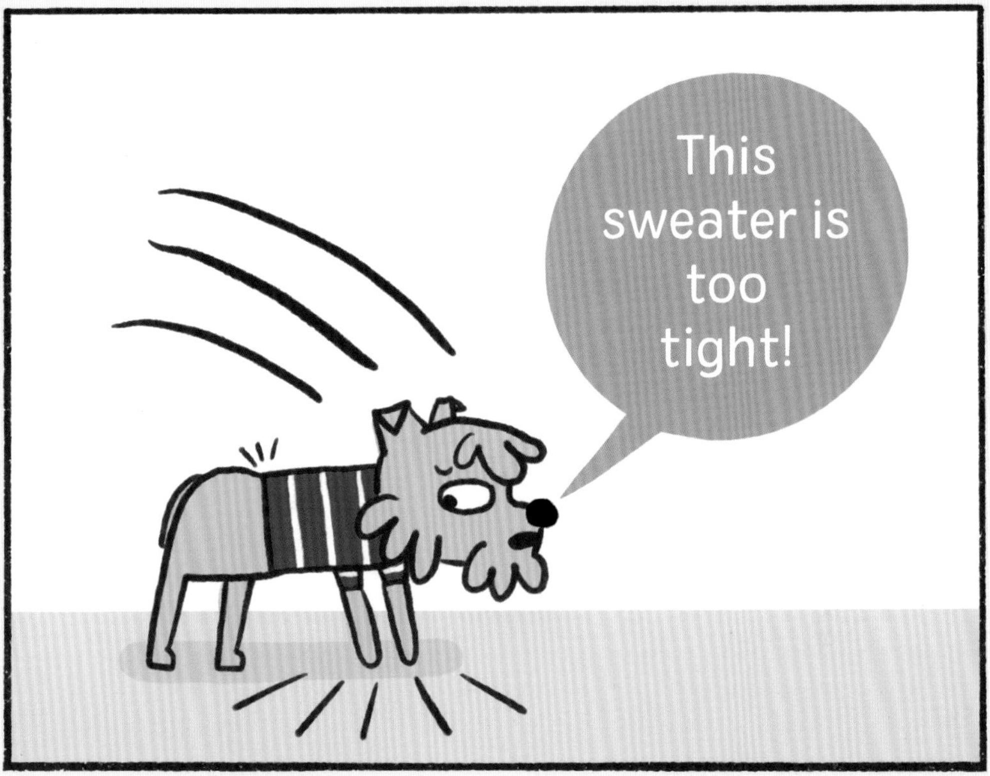
This sweater is too tight!

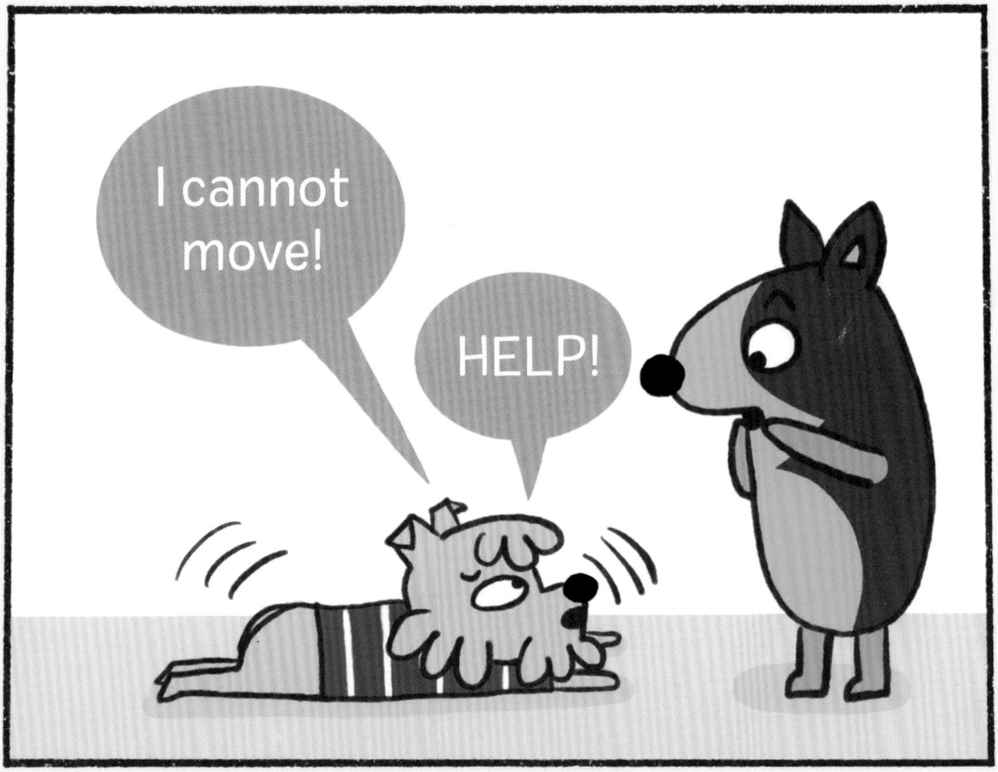
I cannot move!
HELP!

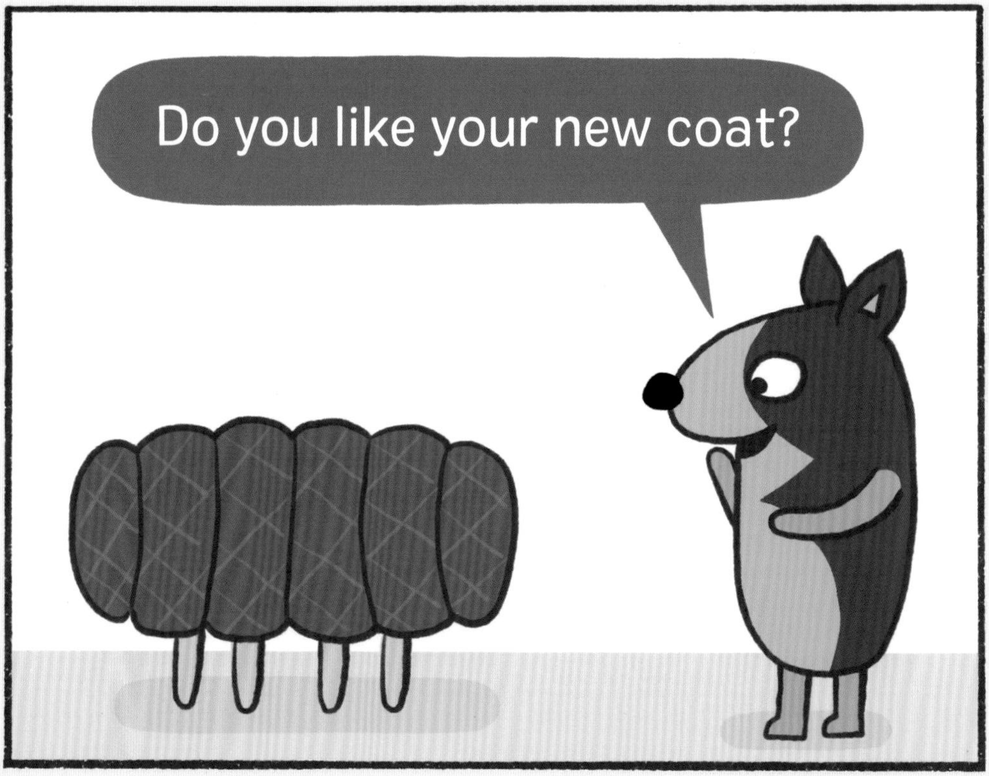
Do you like your new coat?

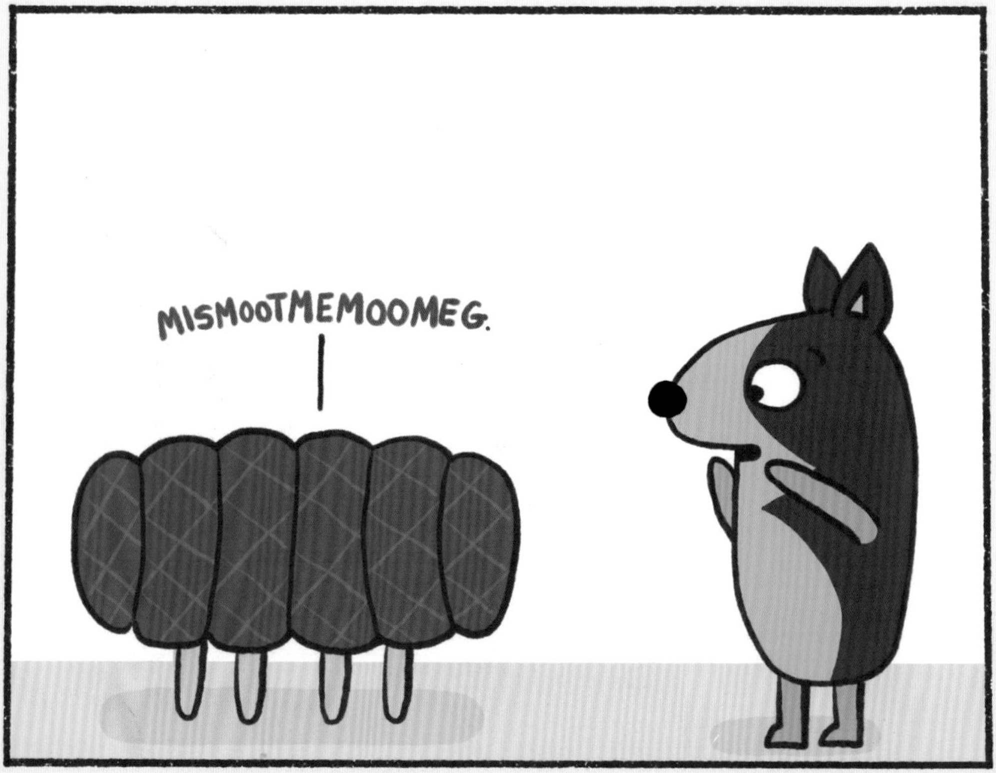
MISMOOTMEMOOMEG.

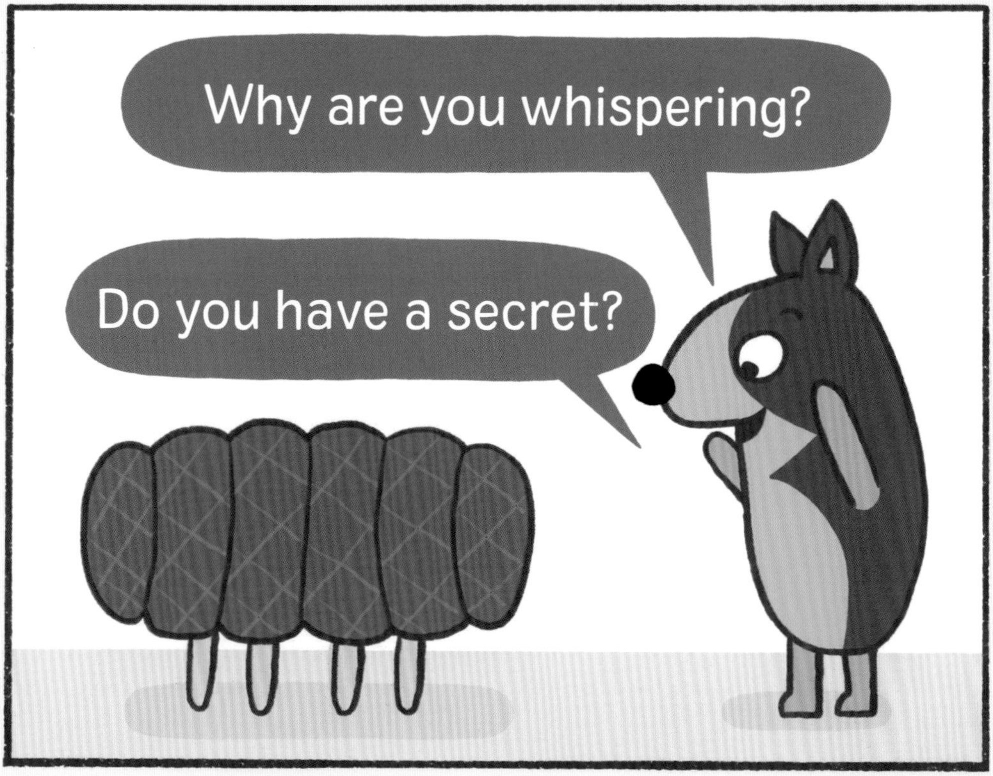
Why are you whispering?
Do you have a secret?

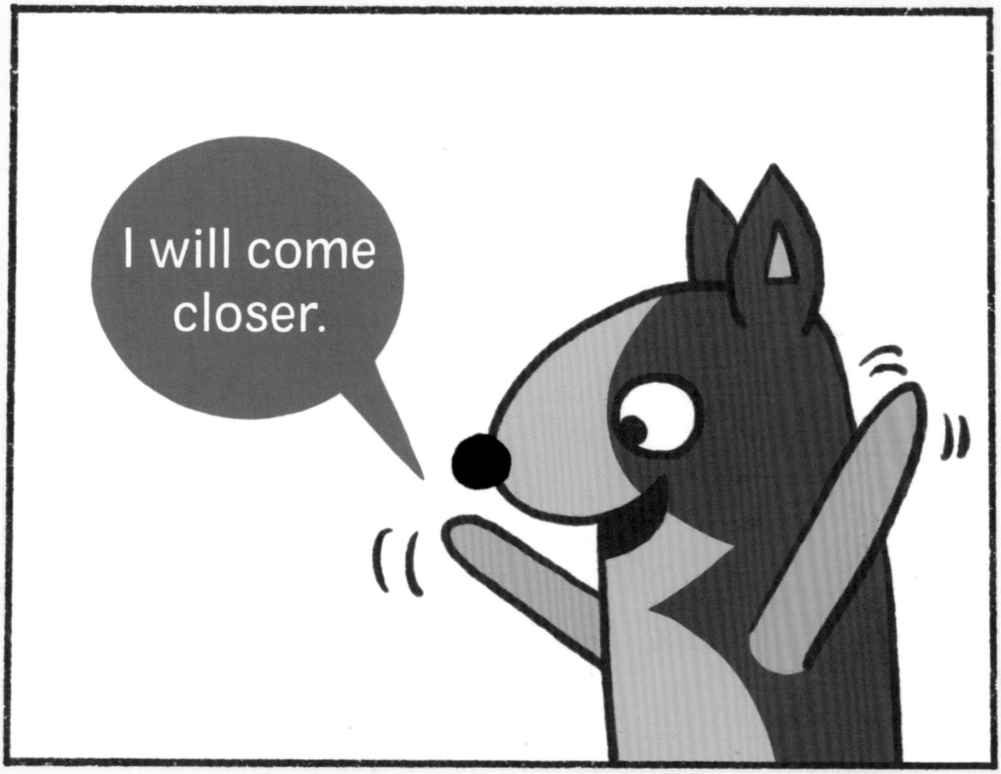
I will come closer.

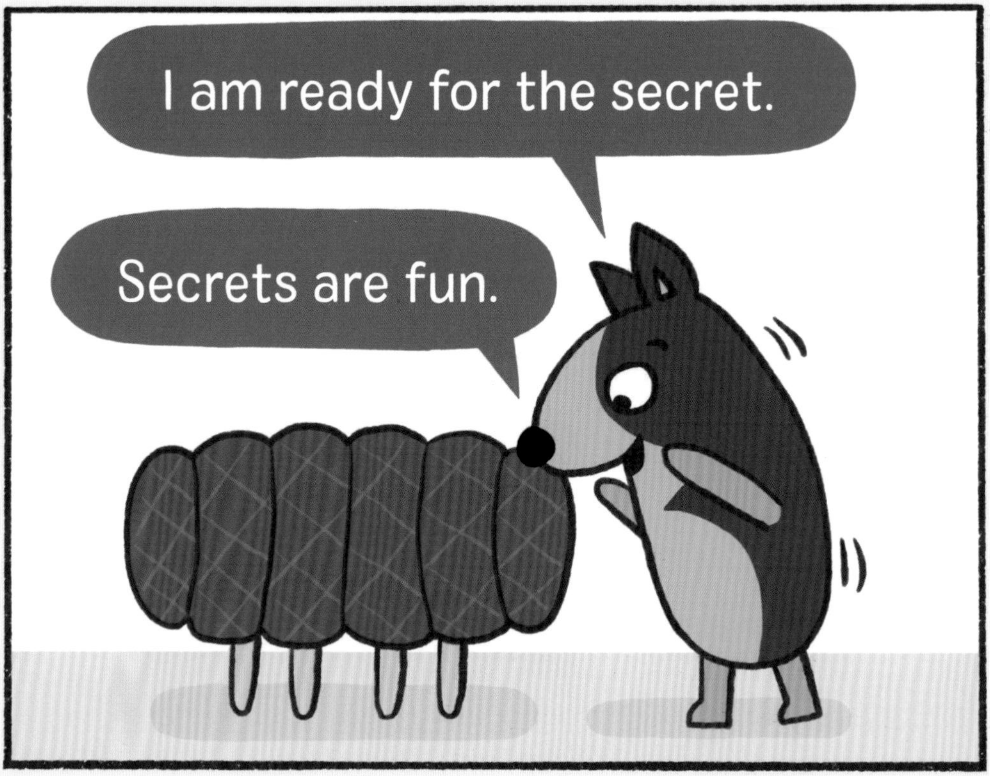
I am ready for the secret.
Secrets are fun.

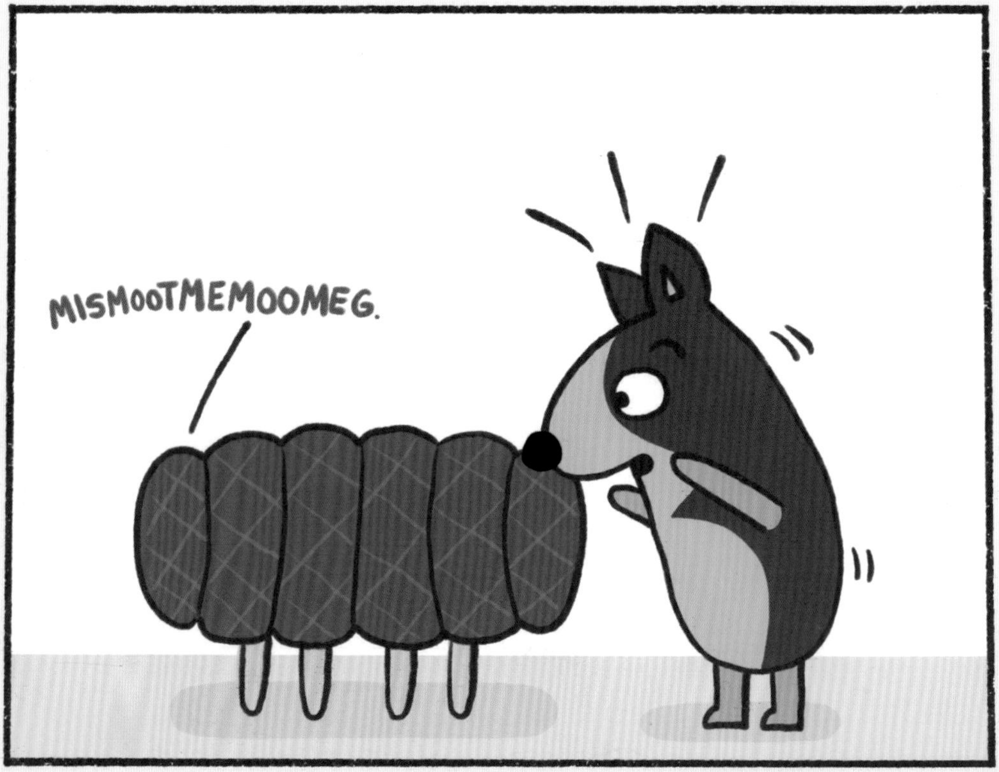
MISMOOTMEMOOMEG.

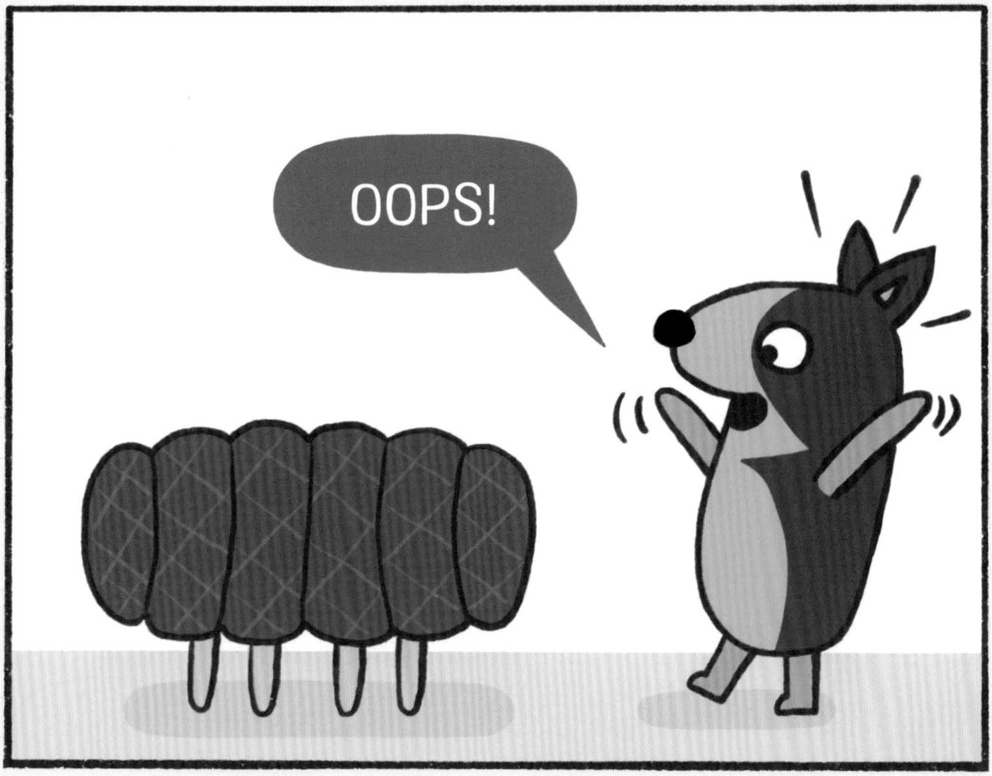
OOPS!

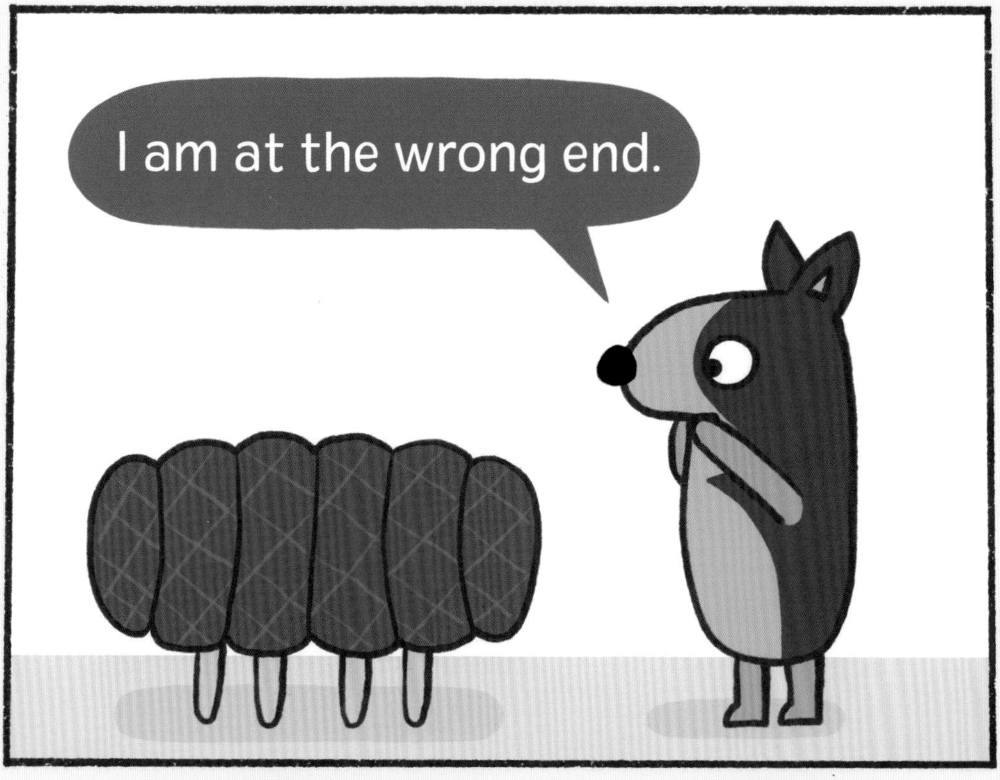
I am at the wrong end.

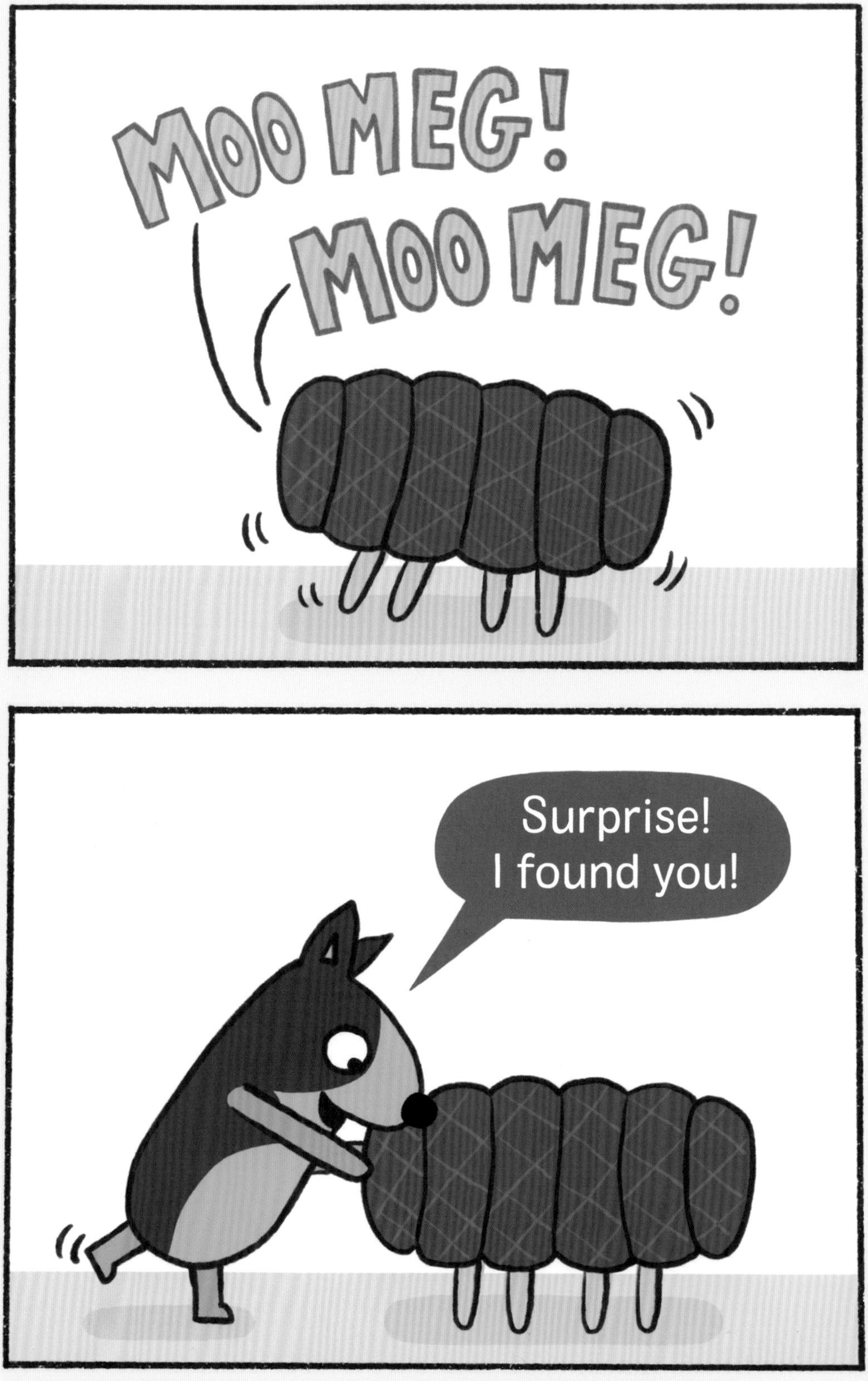
MOO MEG!
MOO MEG!
Surprise!
I found you!

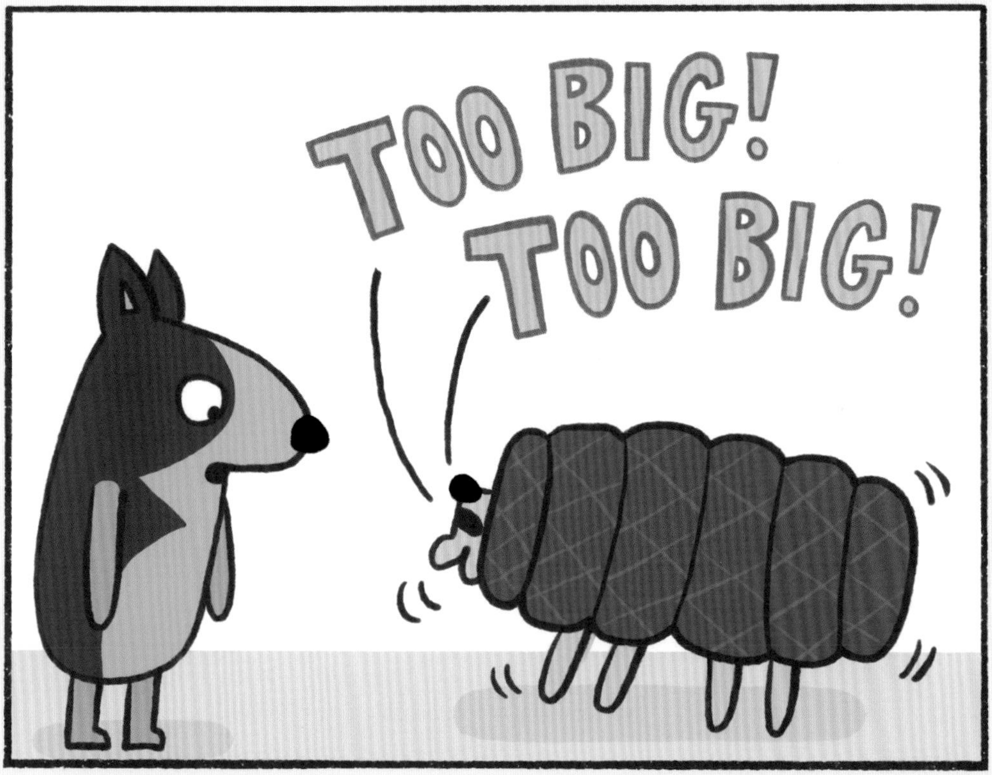
TOO BIG! TOO BIG!

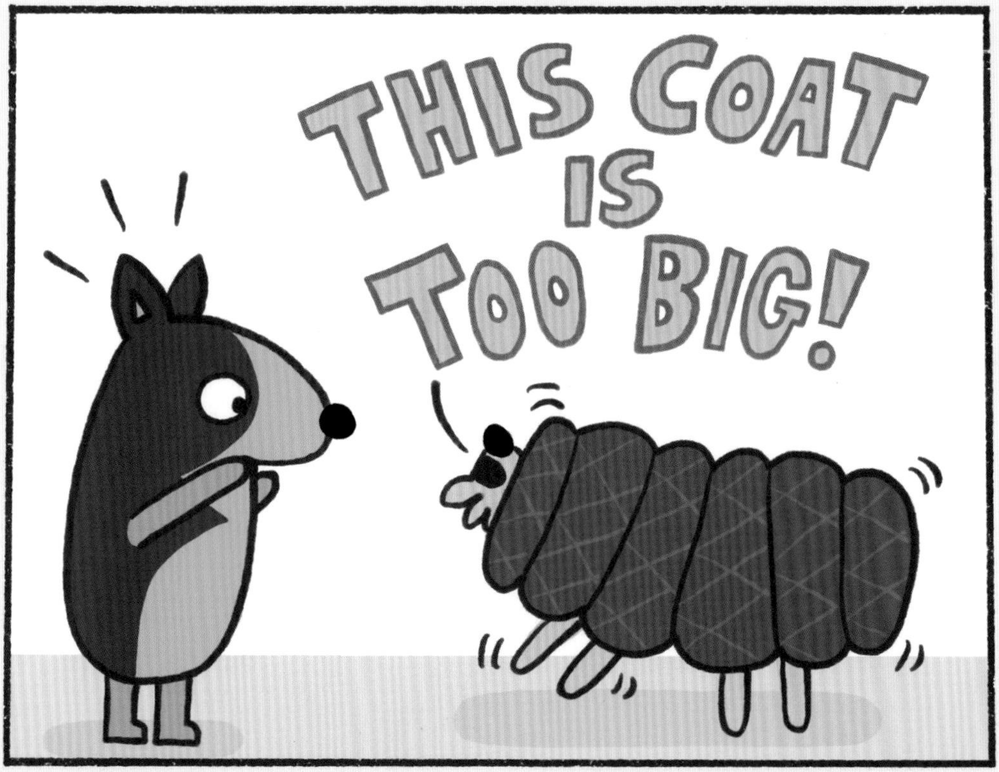
THIS COAT IS TOO BIG!

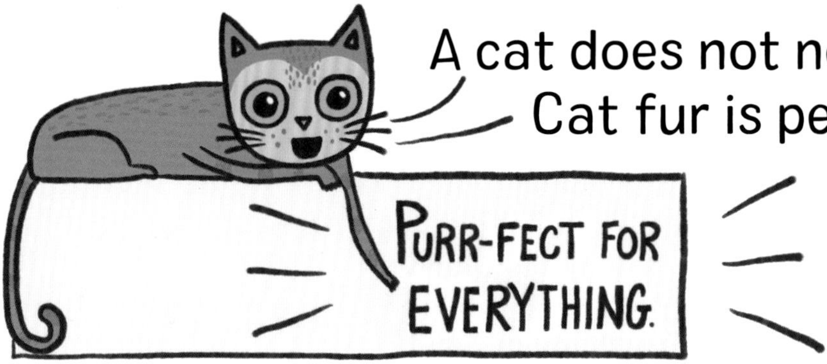
PURR-FECT FOR EVERYTHING.

A cat does not need a coat.
Cat fur is perfect!

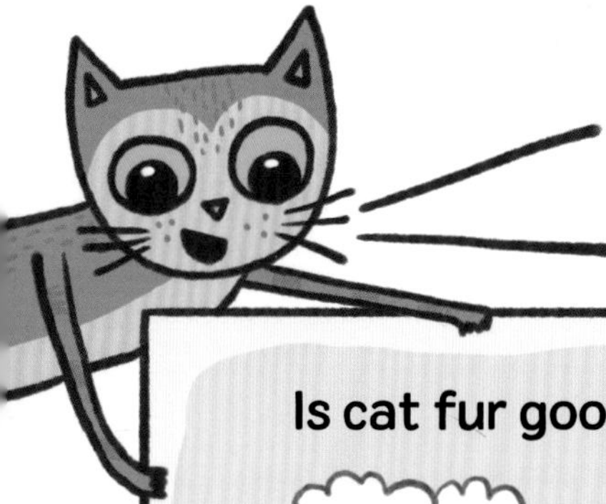

Cats are curious.

They ask questions.

Is cat fur good for rain?

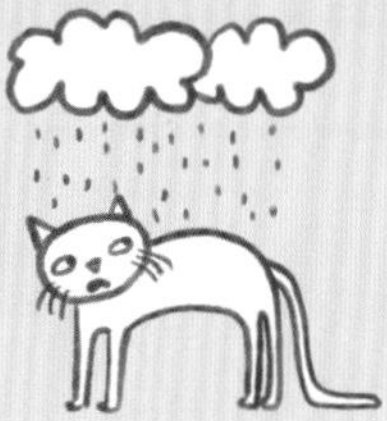

- [x] YES
- [ ] NO

Is cat fur good for snow?

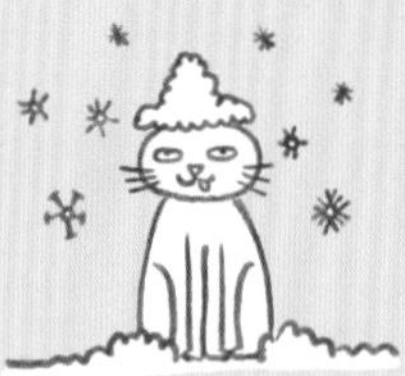

- [x] YES
- [ ] NO

Is cat fur good for wind?

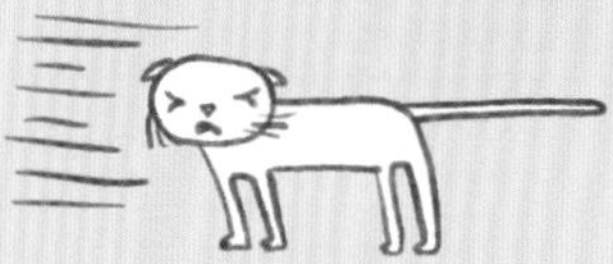

- [x] YES
- [ ] NO

Is cat fur good for sun?

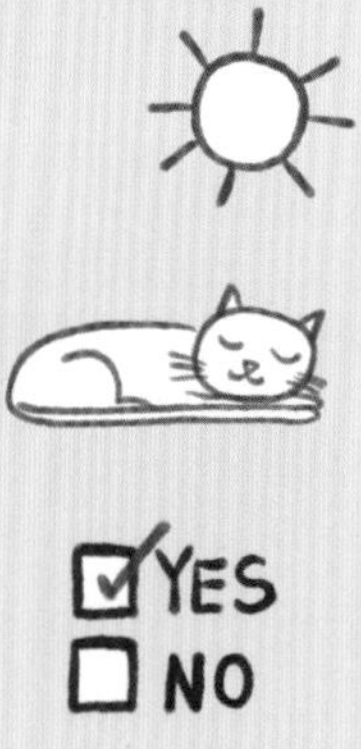

- [x] YES
- [ ] NO

Sharing is fun.

I leave fur everywhere I go...

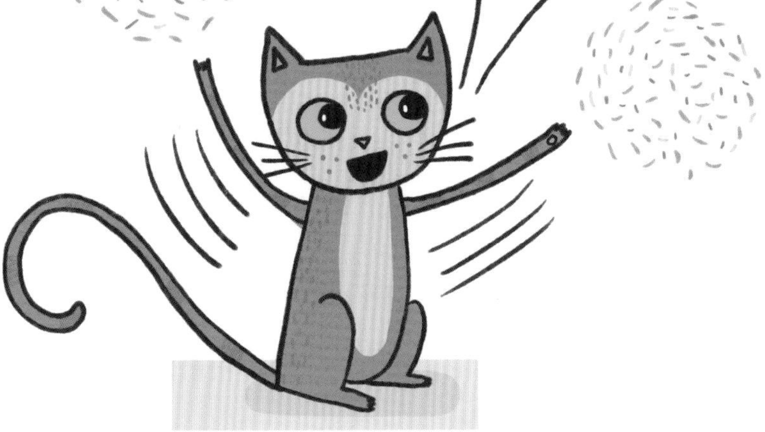

BECAUSE

cats are the best,

AND

the world needs more cat fur!

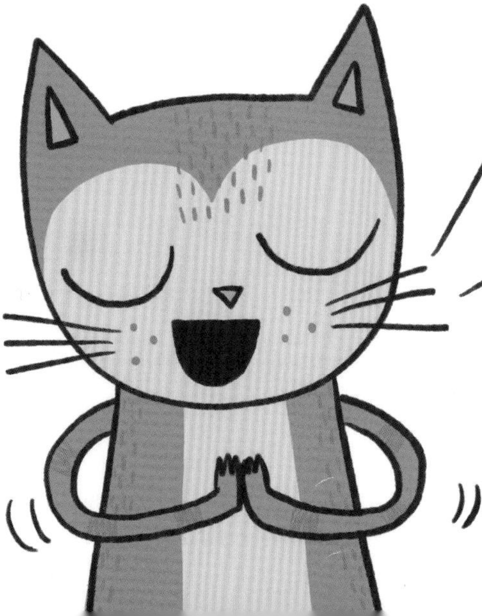

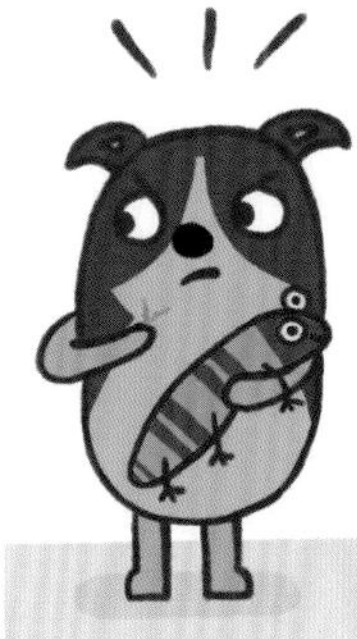

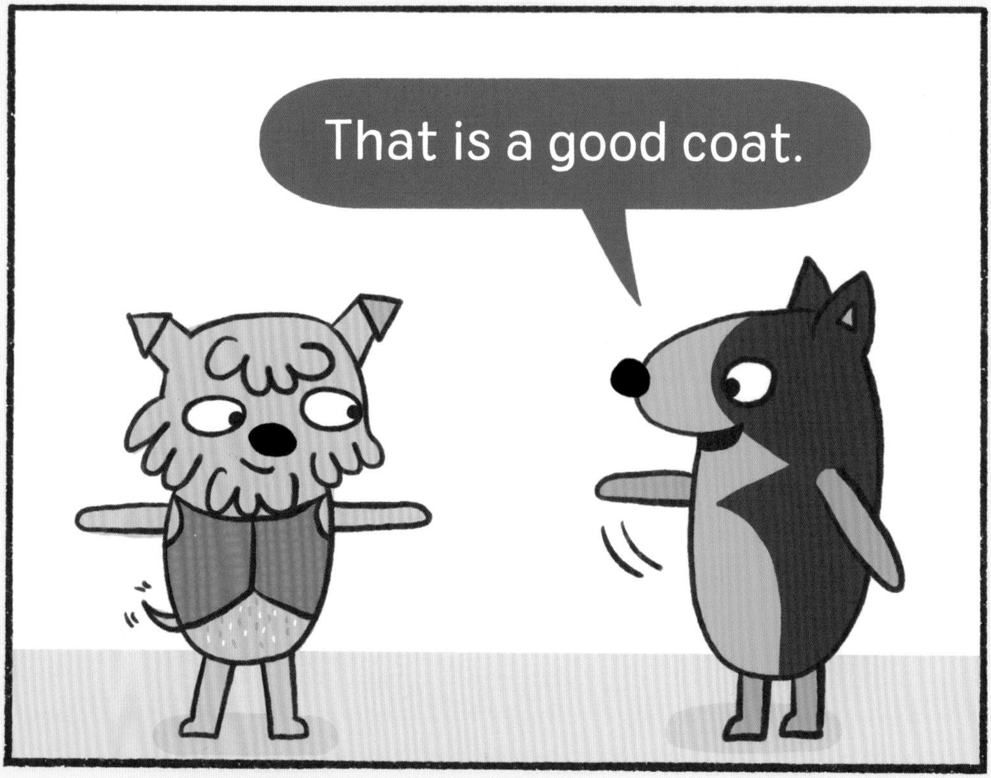
That is a good coat.

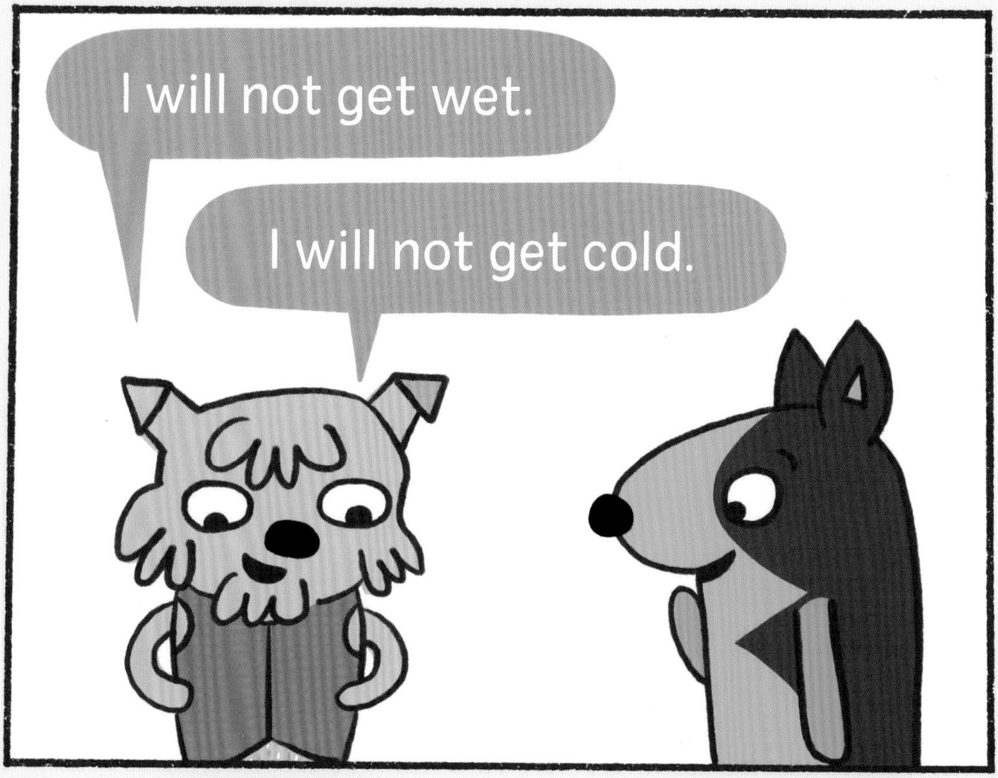
I will not get wet.
I will not get cold.

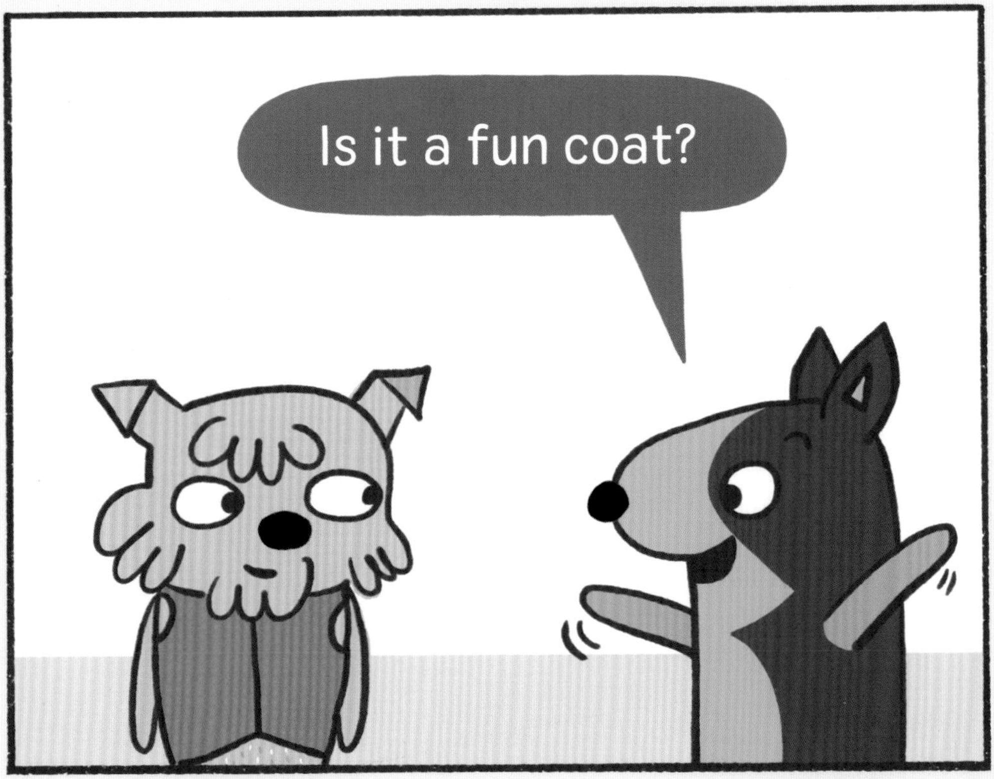
Is it a fun coat?

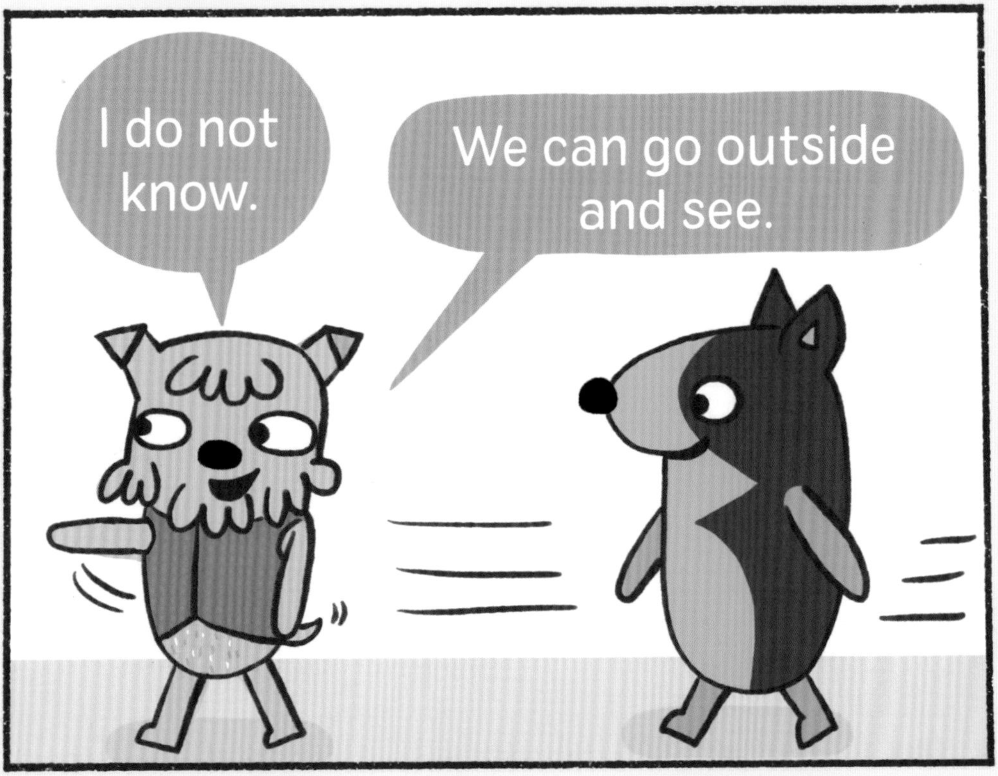
I do not know.
We can go outside and see.

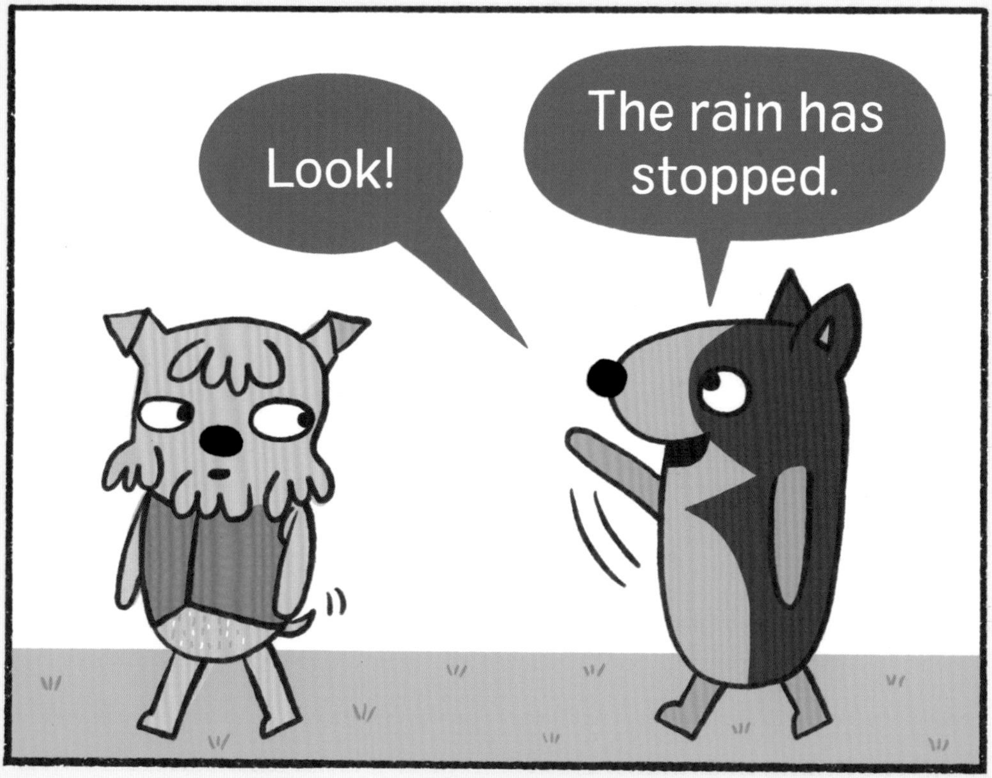
Look!
The rain has stopped.

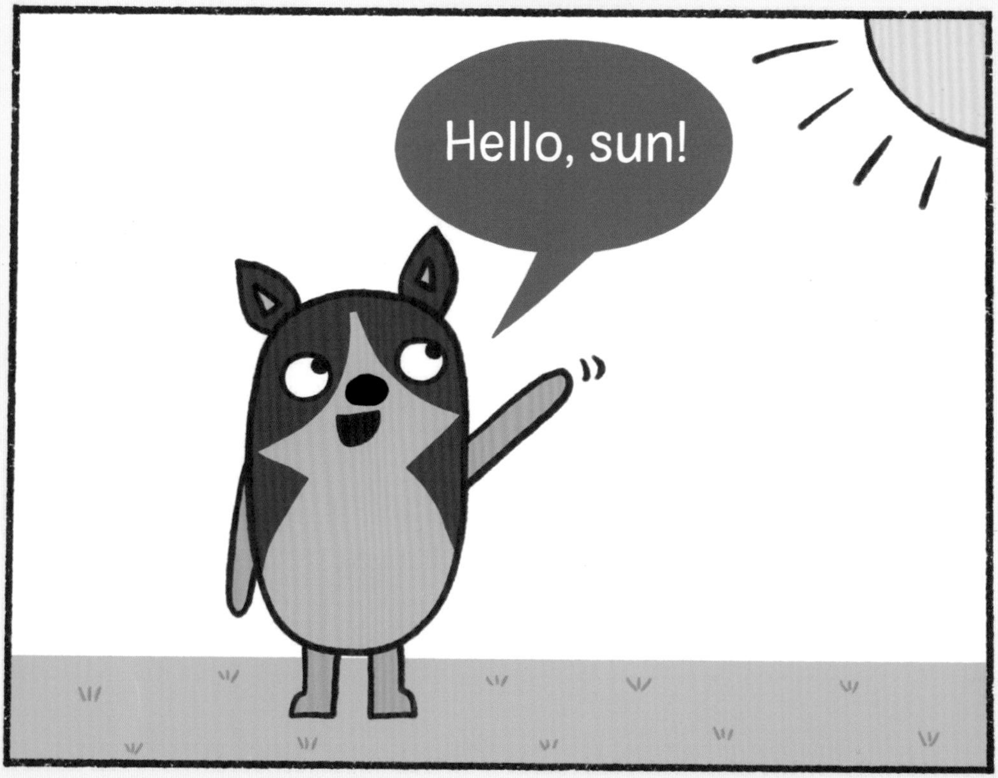
Hello, sun!

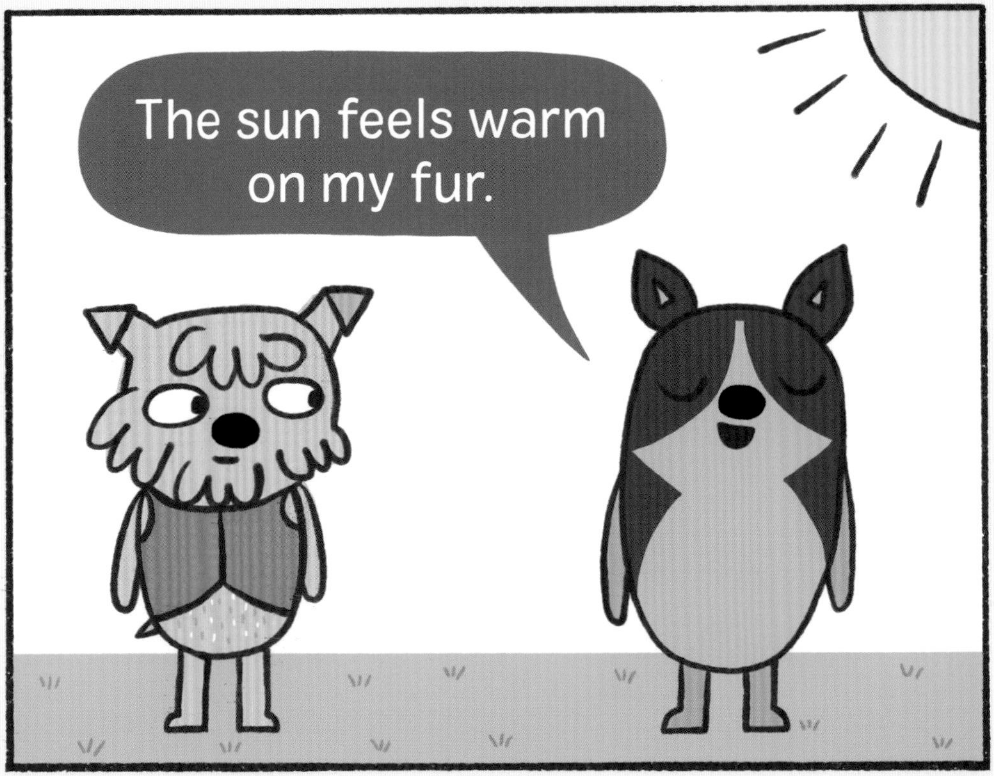
The sun feels warm on my fur.

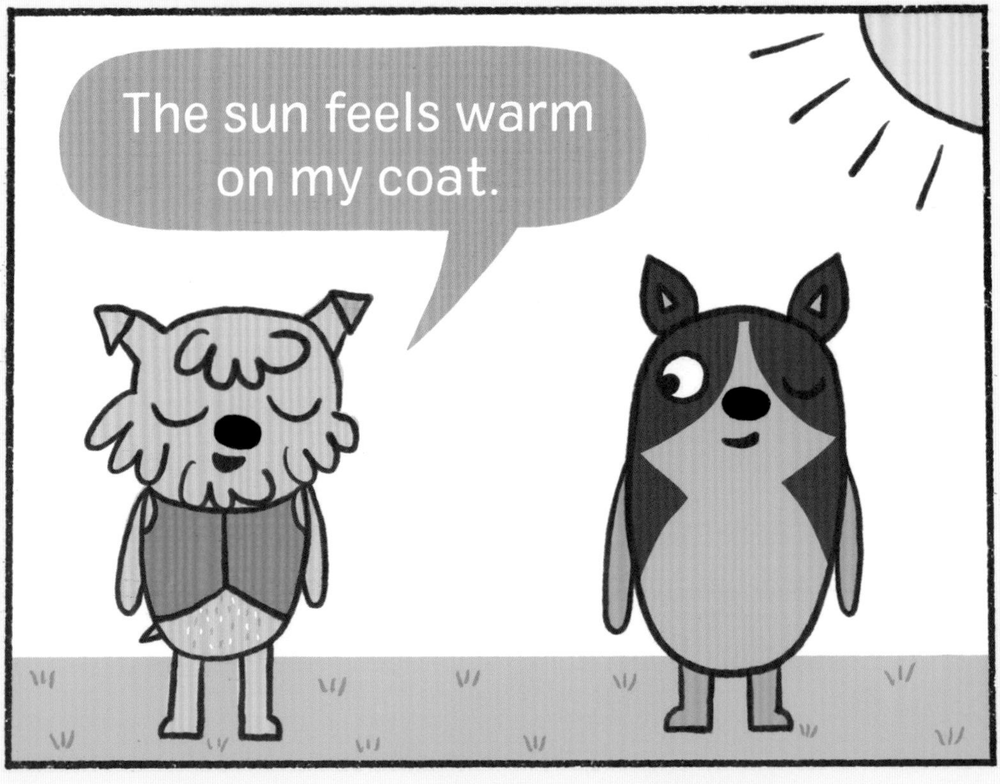
The sun feels warm on my coat.

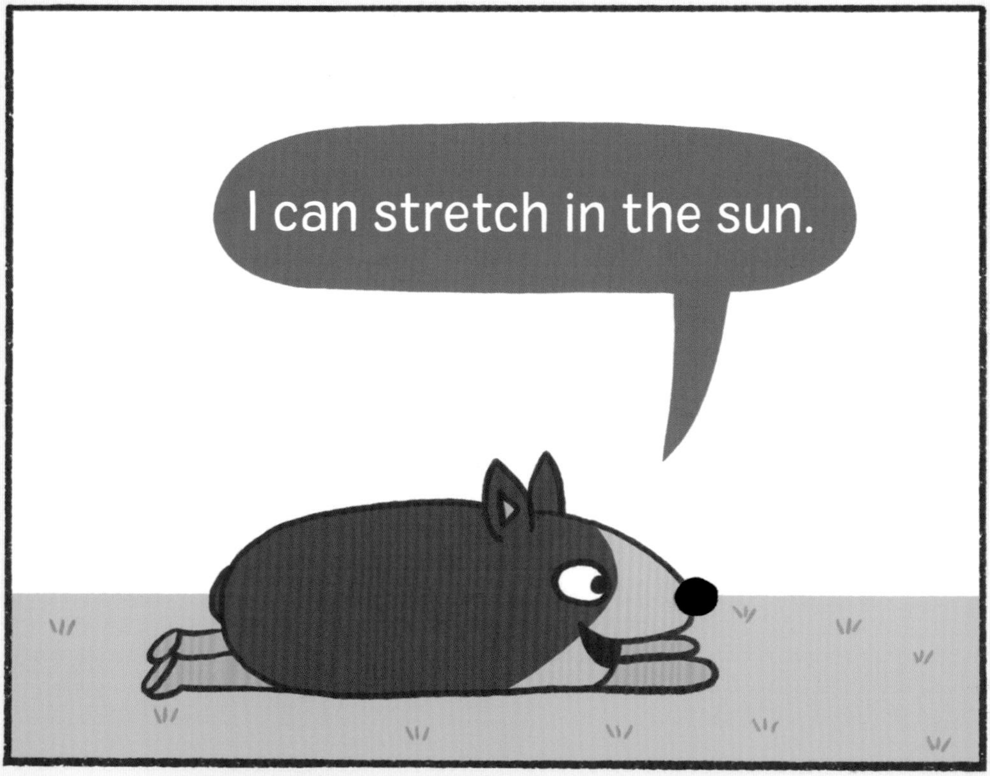
I can stretch in the sun.

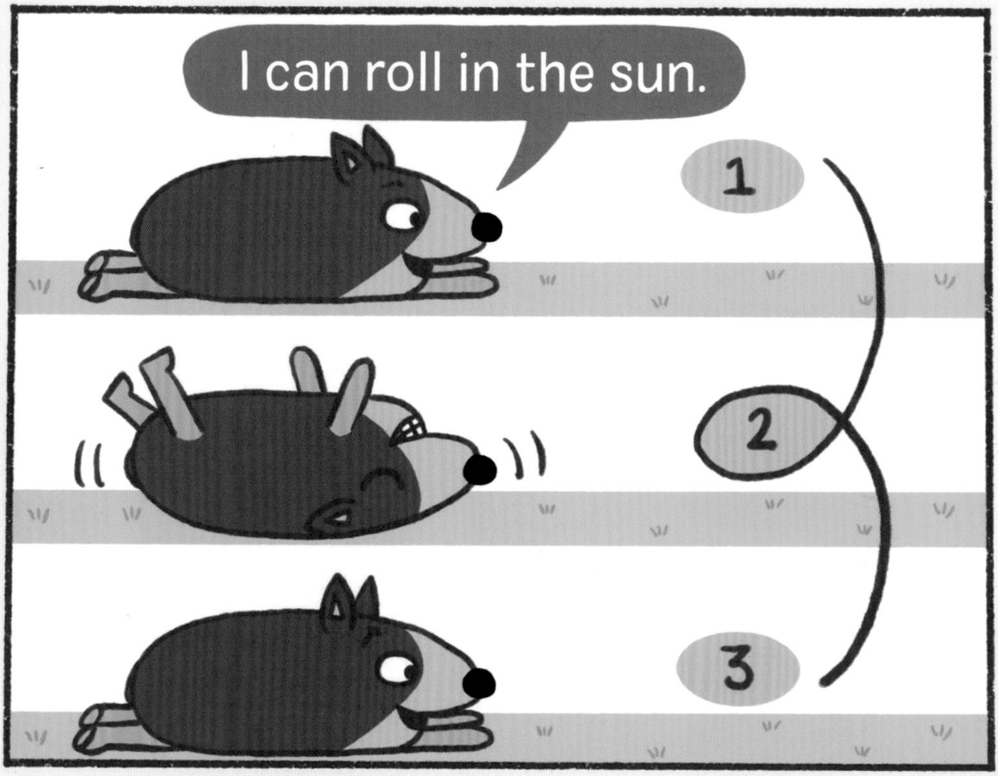
I can roll in the sun.
1
2
3

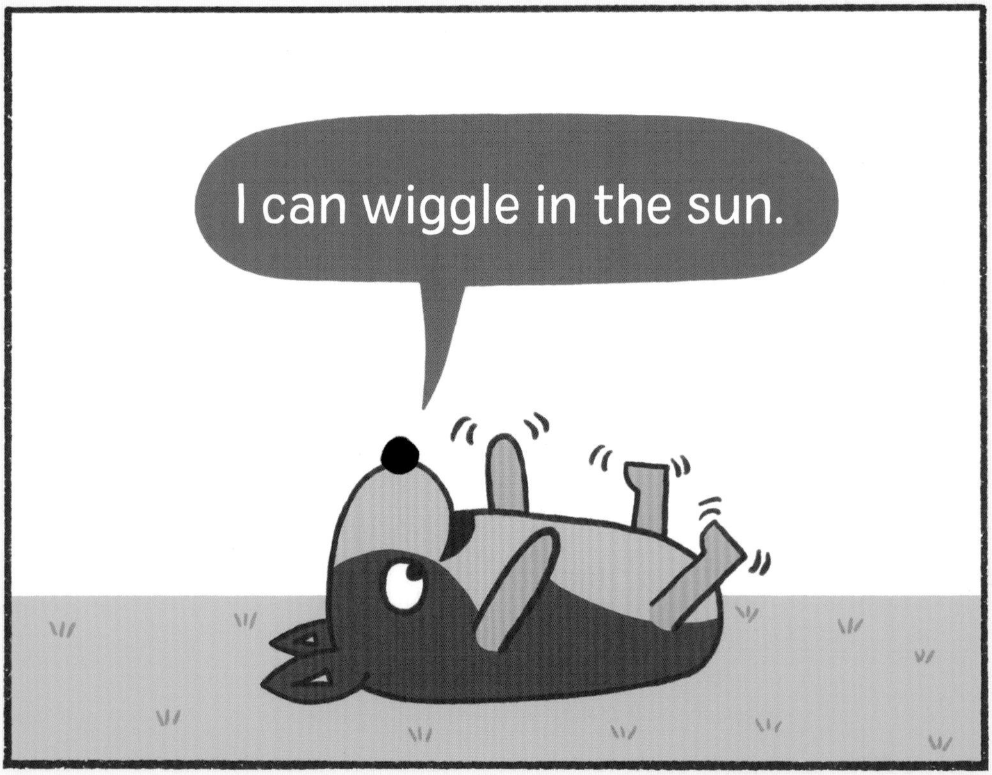
I can wiggle in the sun.

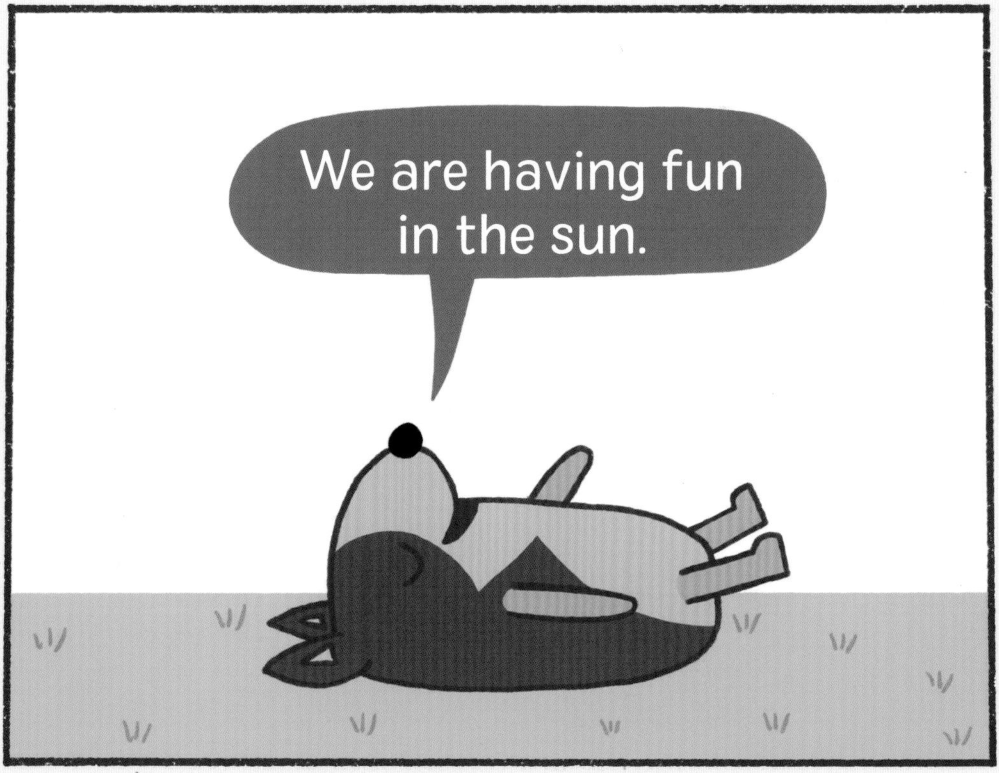
We are having fun
in the sun.

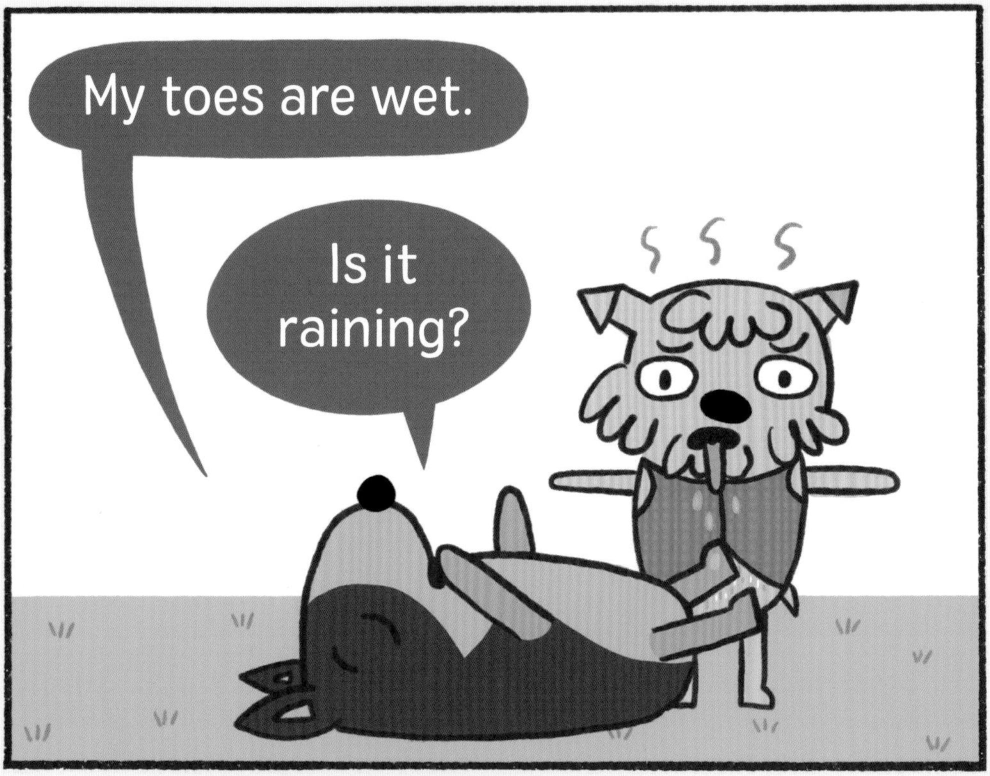
My toes are wet.
Is it raining?

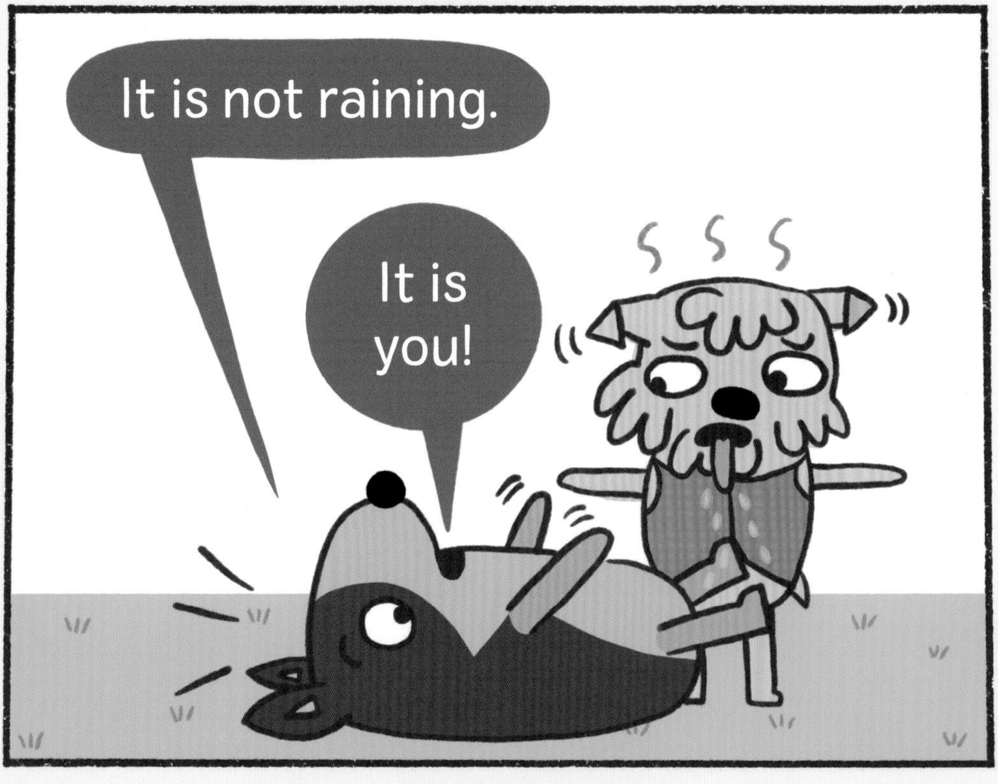
It is not raining.
It is you!

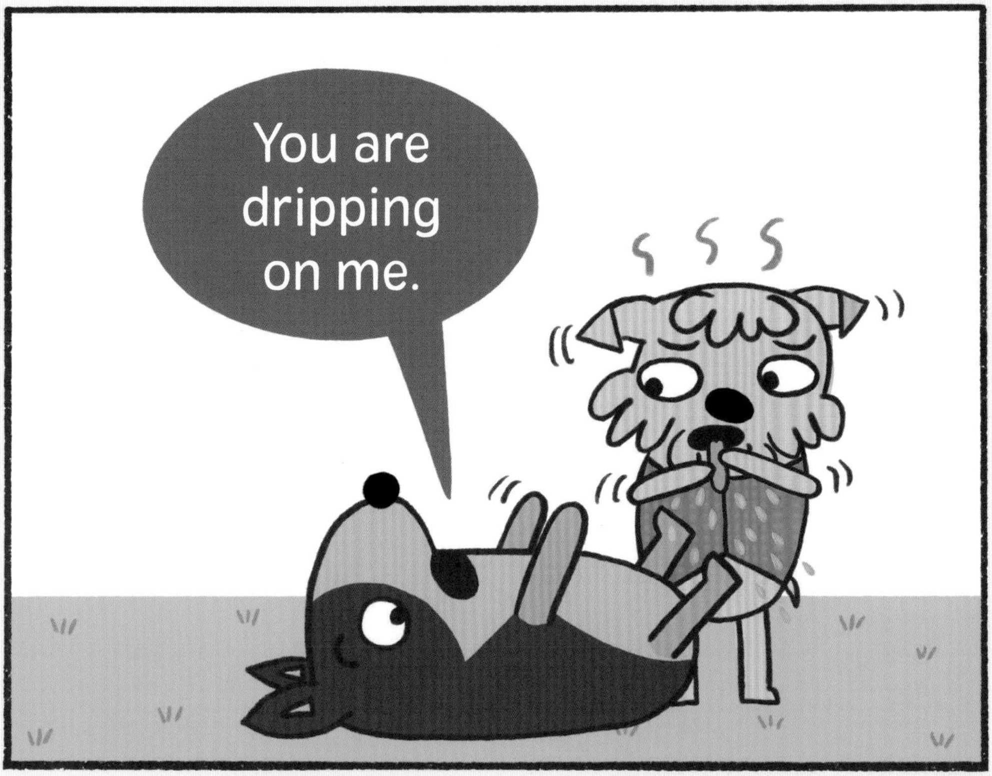
You are dripping on me.

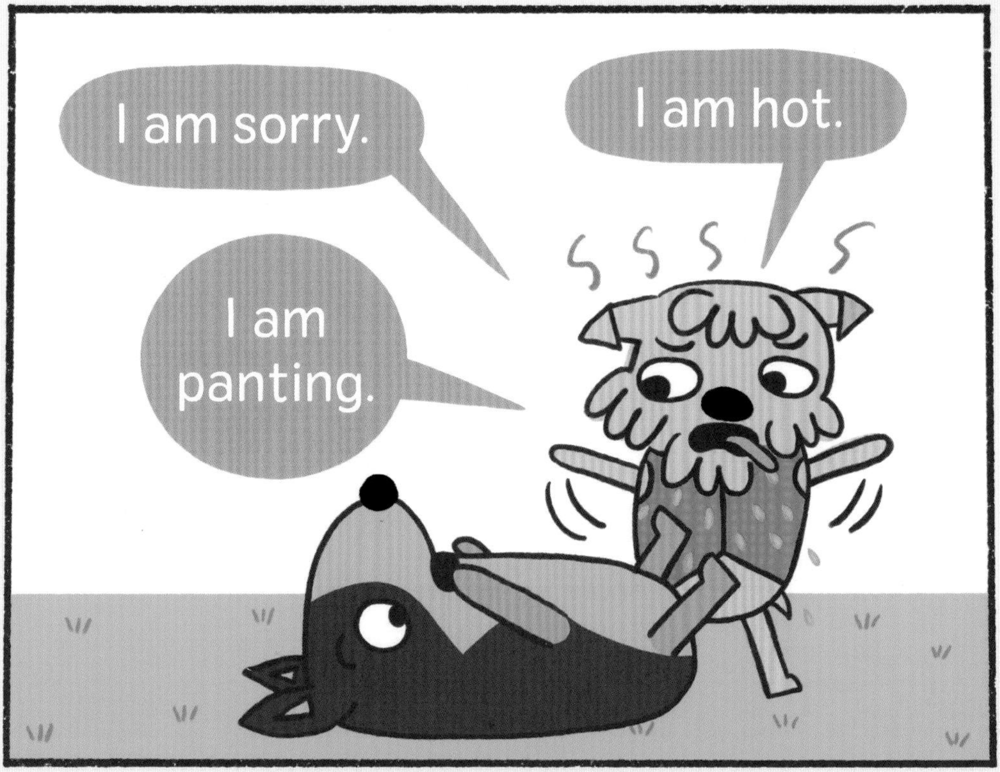
I am sorry.
I am hot.
I am panting.

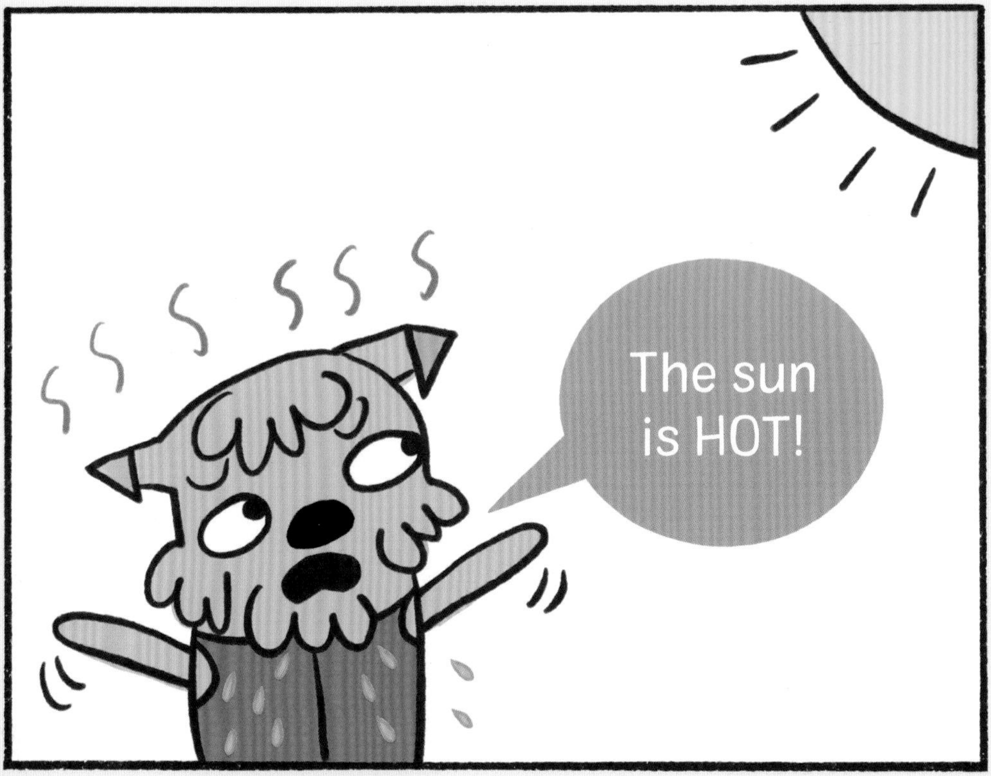
The sun is HOT!

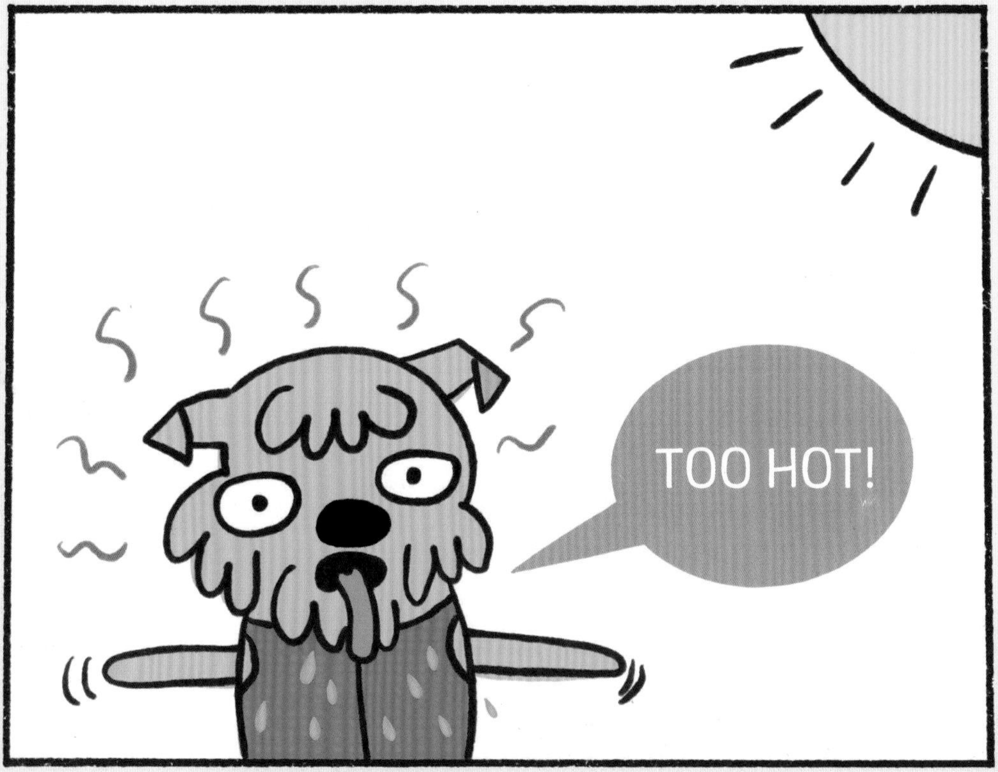
TOO HOT!

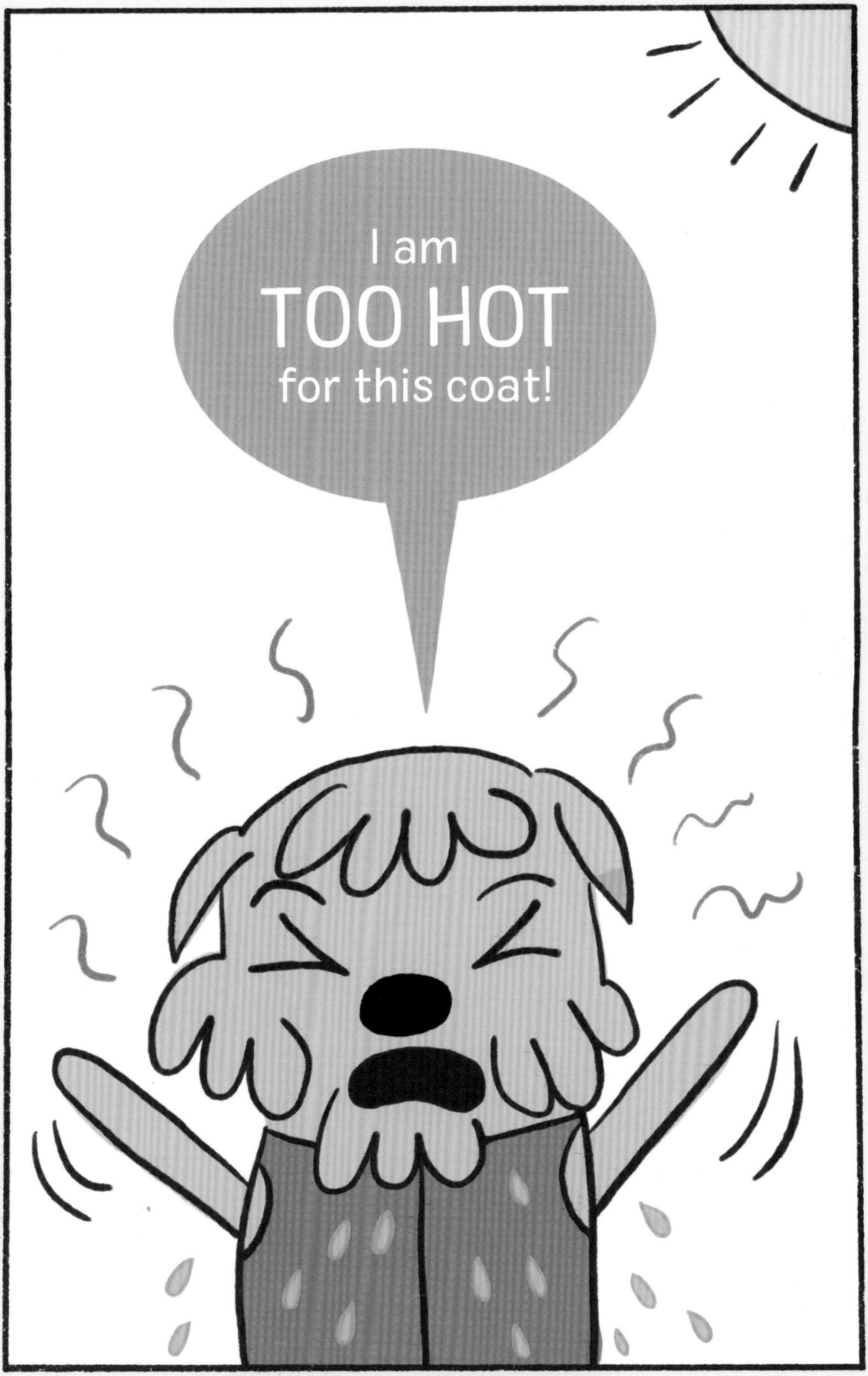
I am
TOO HOT
for this coat!

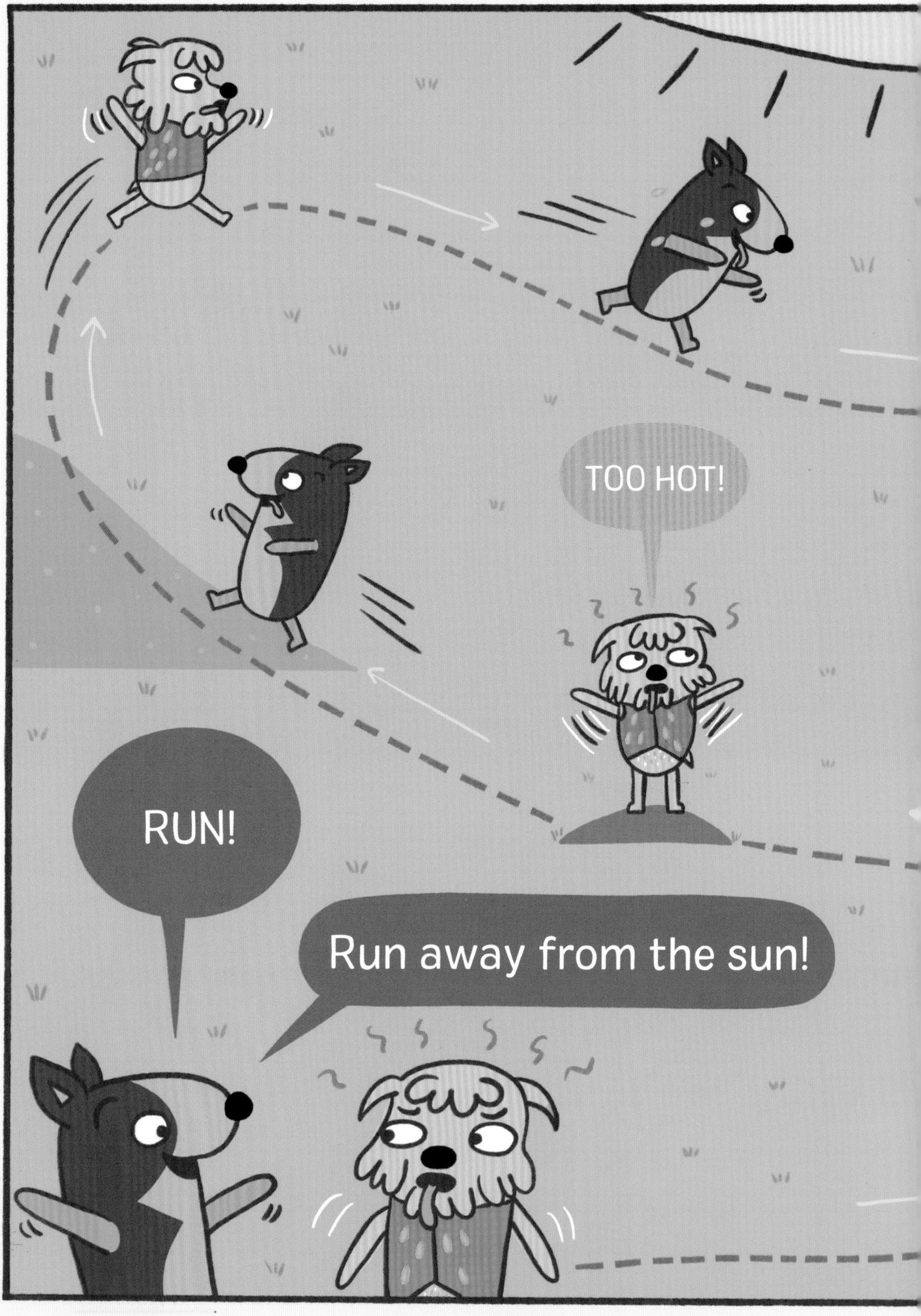
TOO HOT!
RUN!
Run away from the sun!

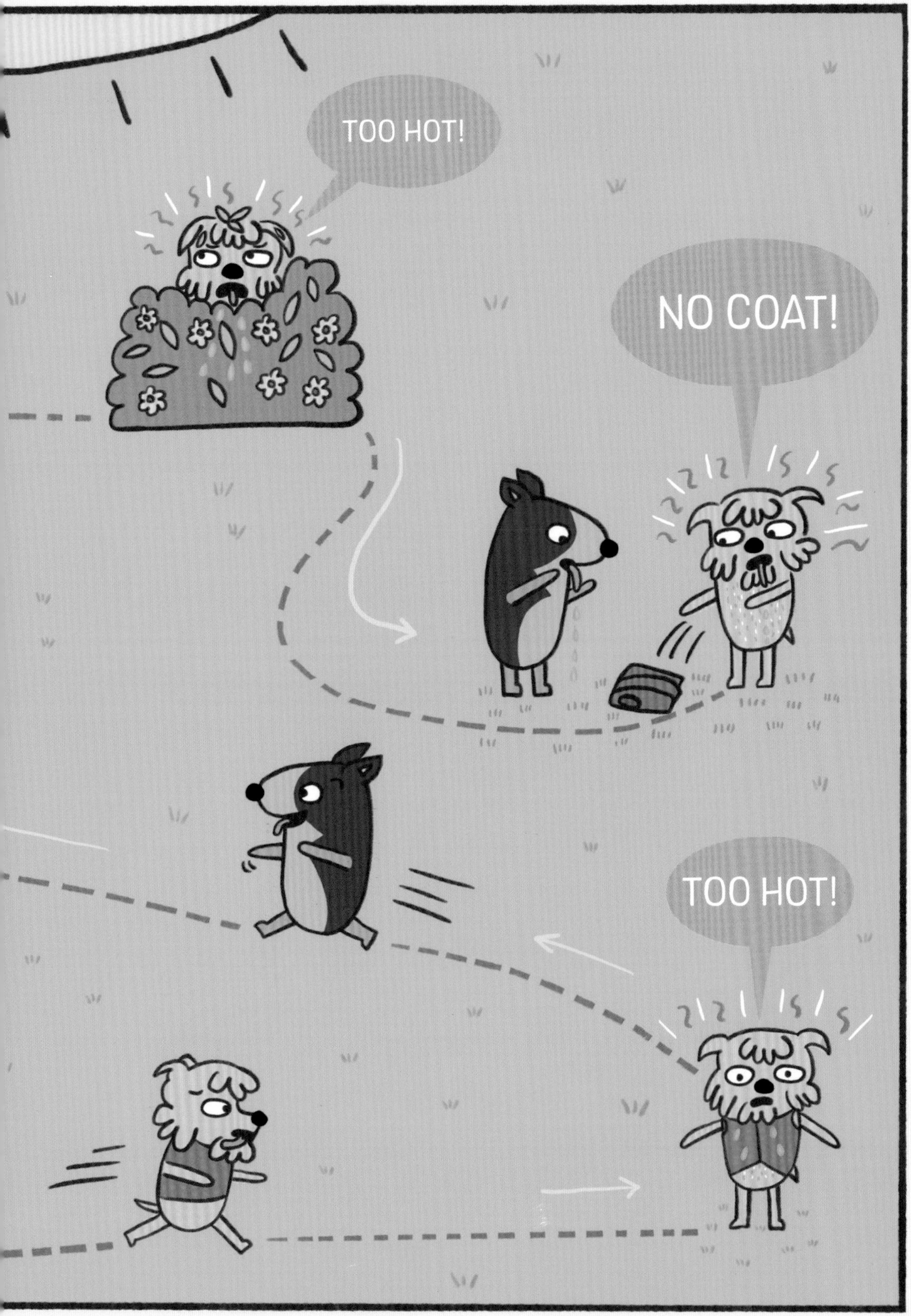
TOO HOT!
NO COAT!
TOO HOT!

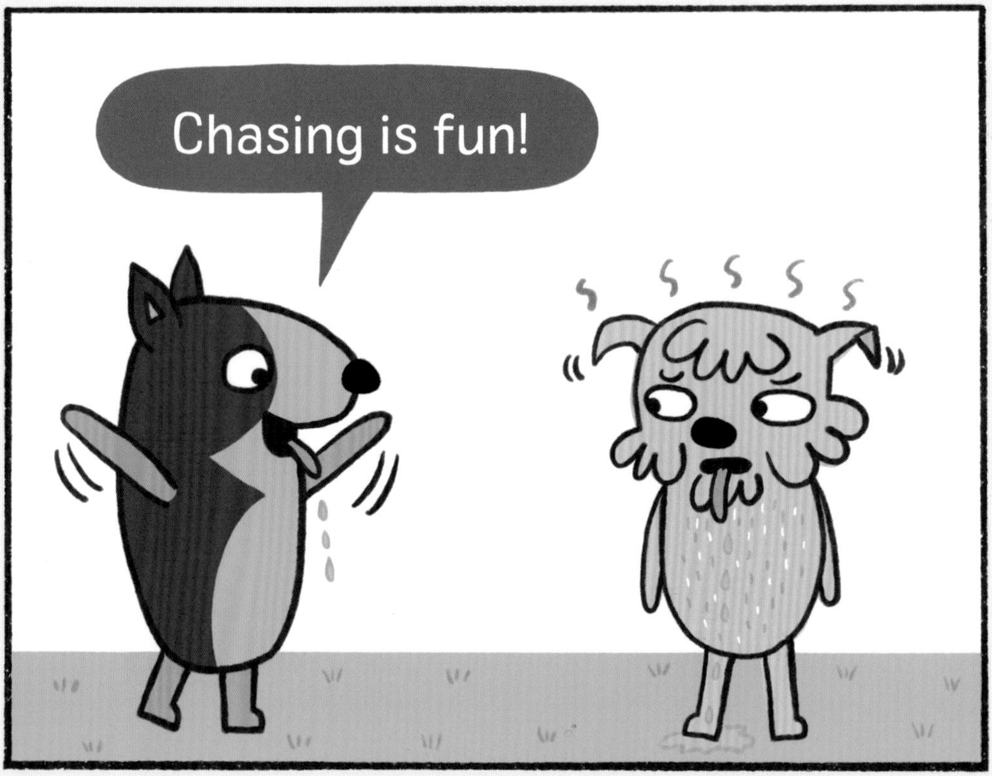
Chasing is fun!

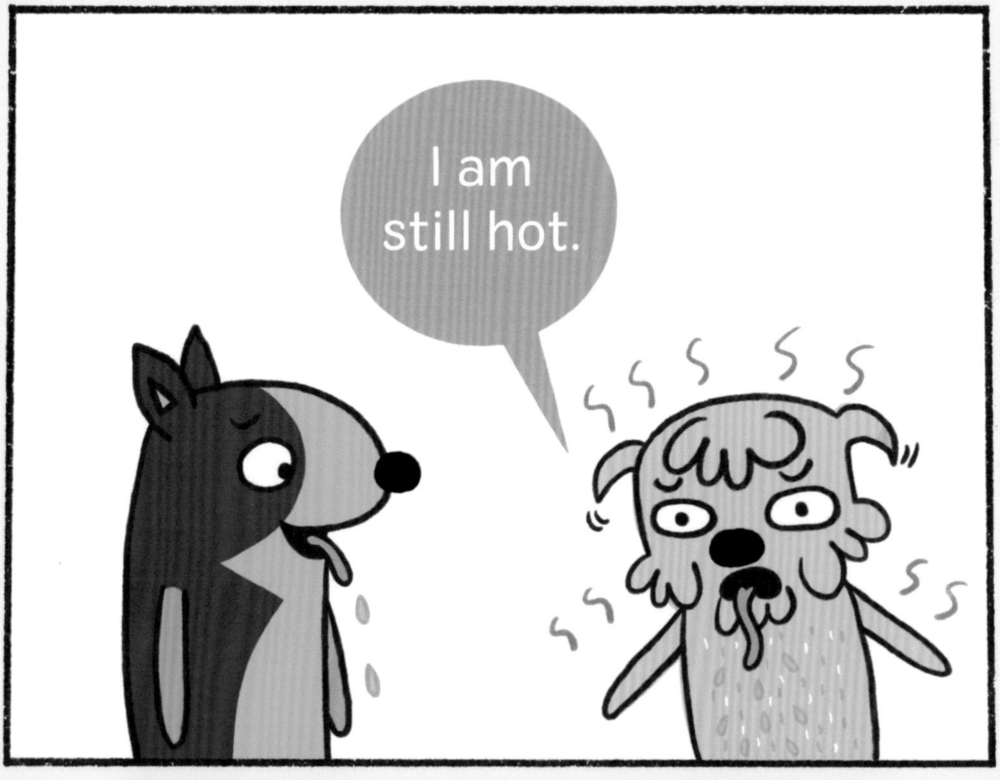
I am still hot.

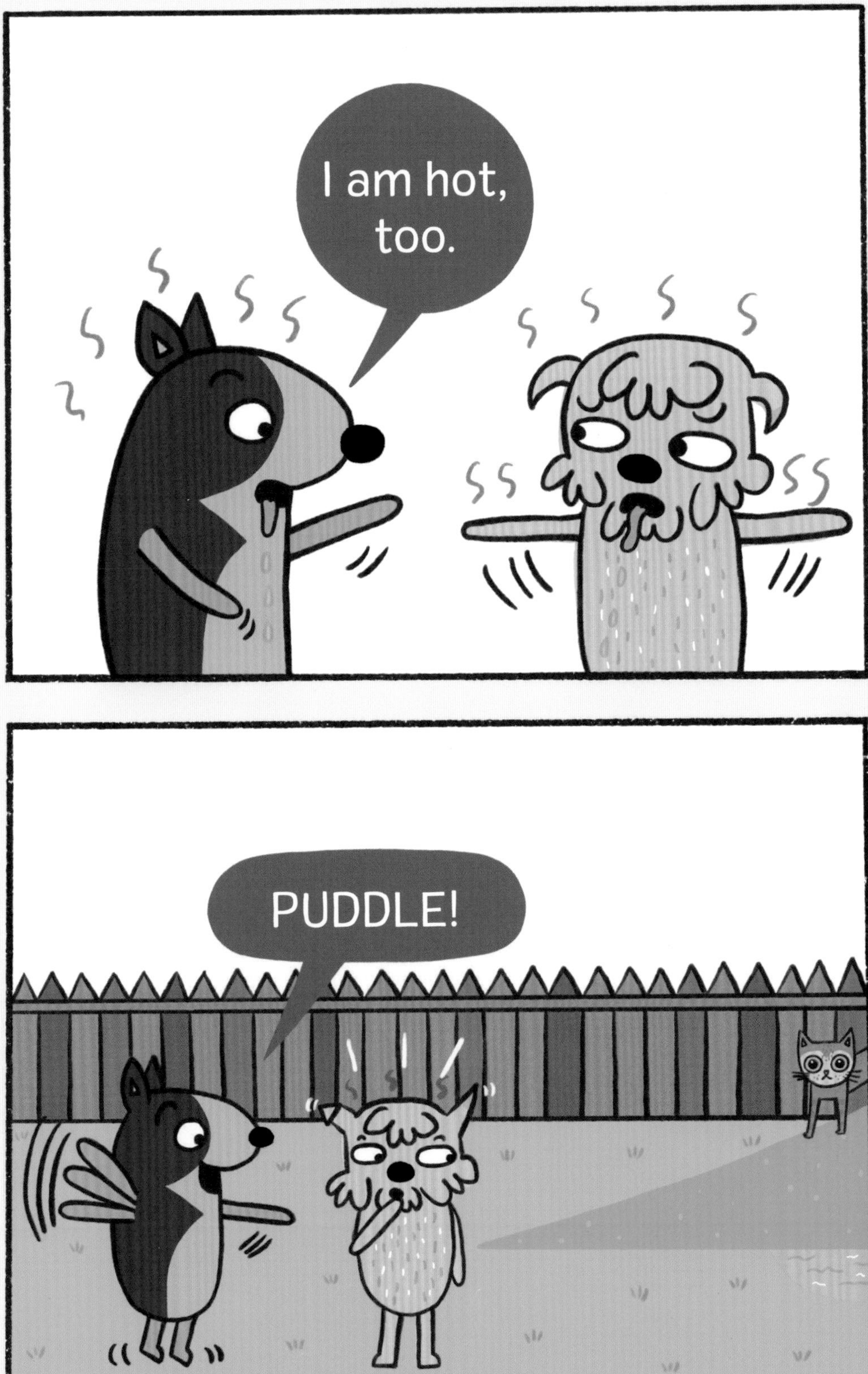
I am hot, too.
PUDDLE!

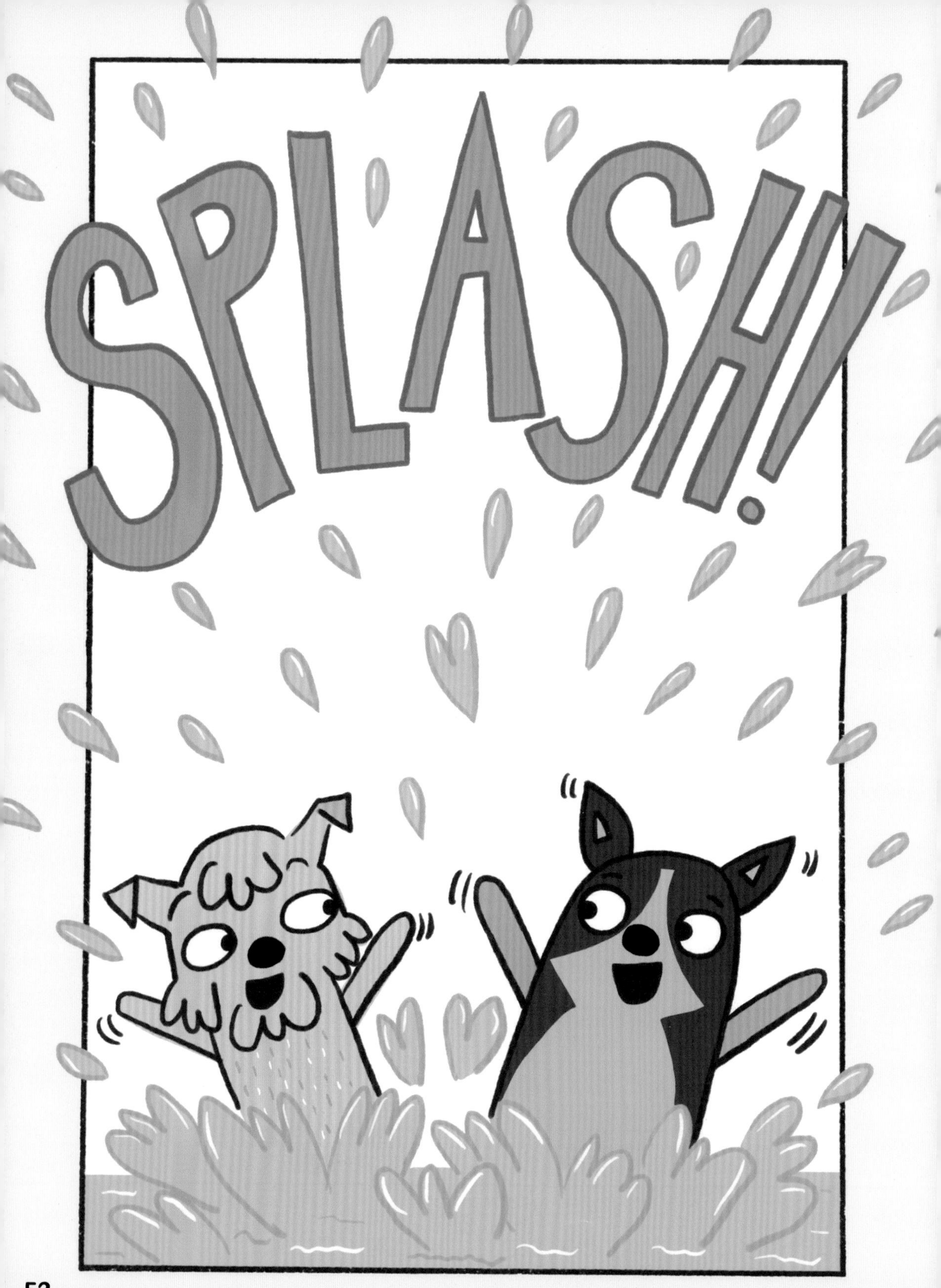
SPLASH!!

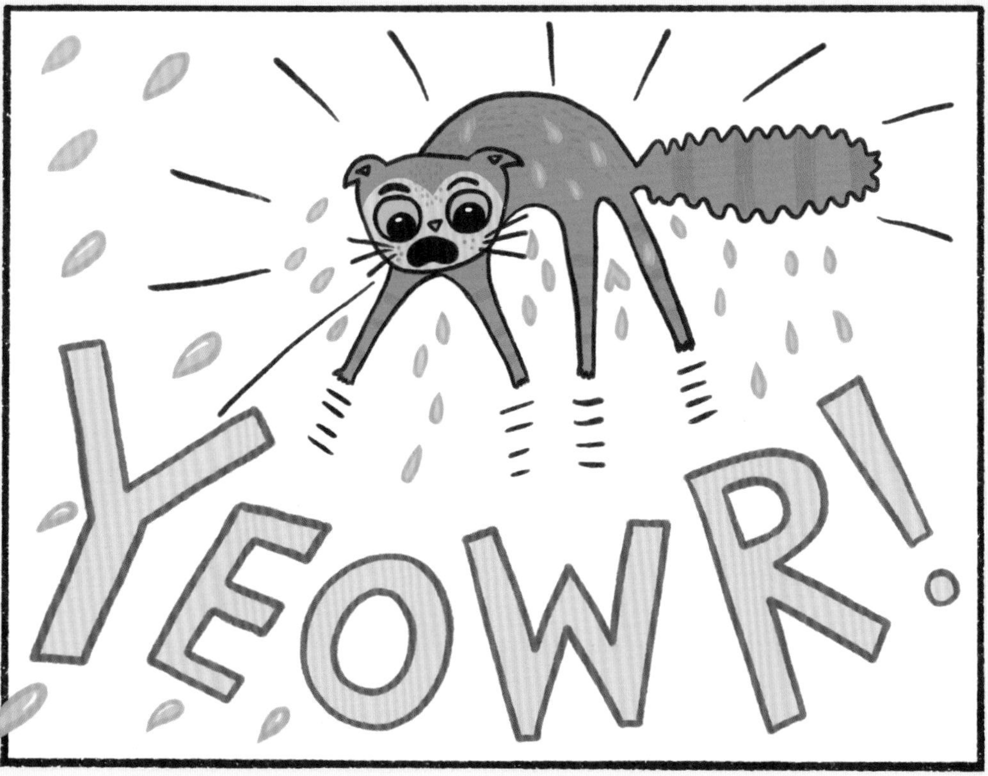
YEOWR!

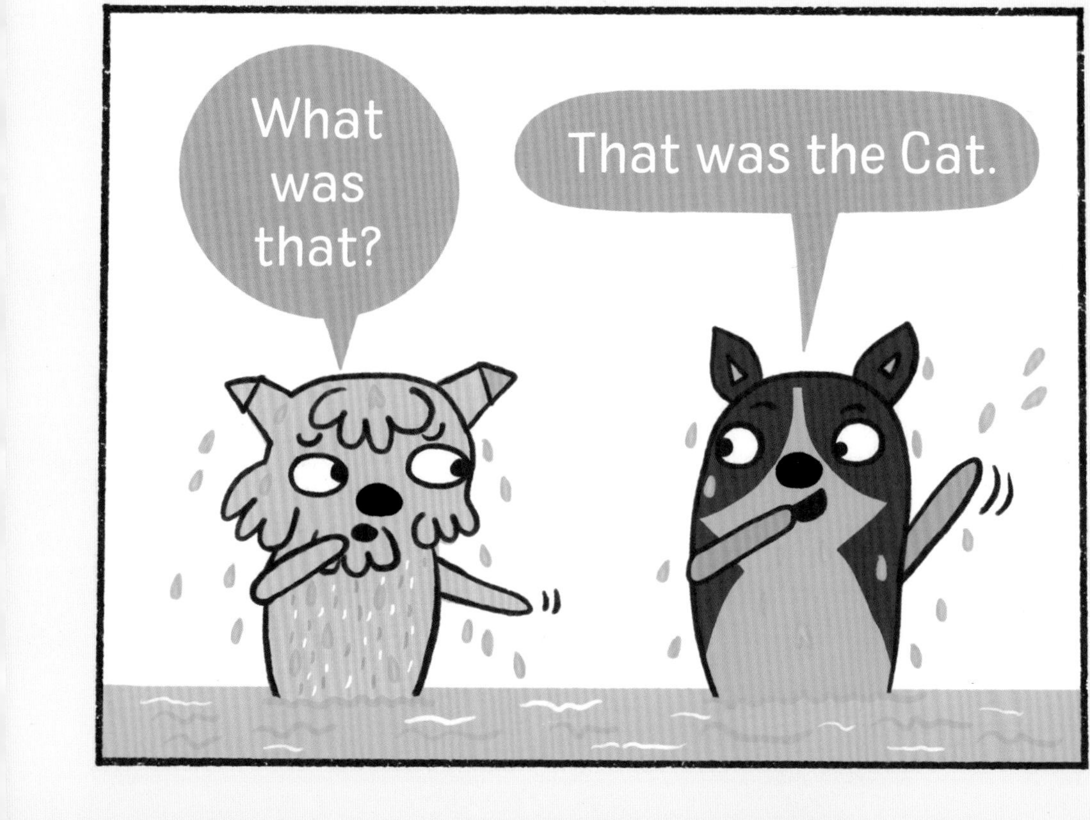
What was that?
That was the Cat.

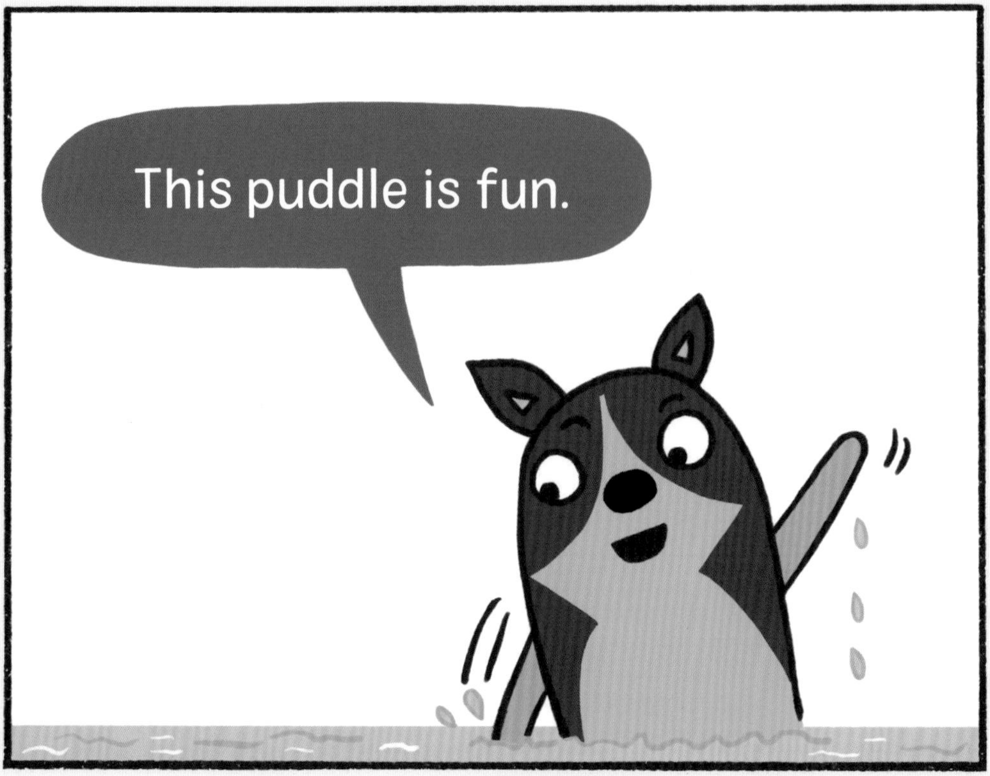
This puddle is fun.

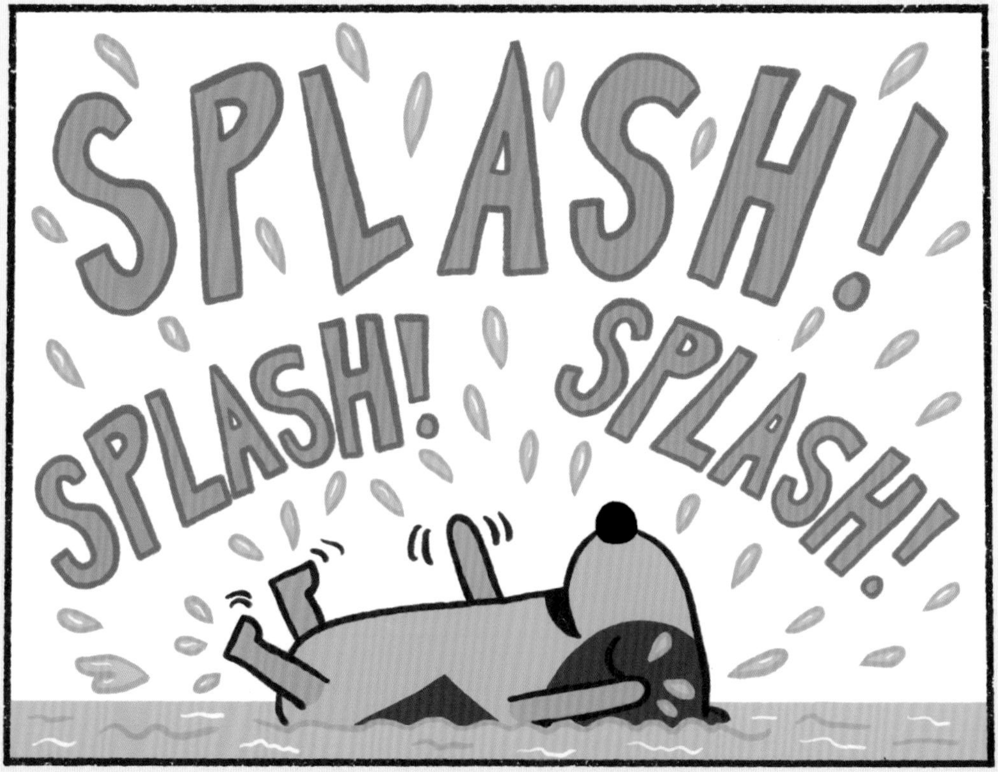
SPLASH!
SPLASH!
SPLASH!

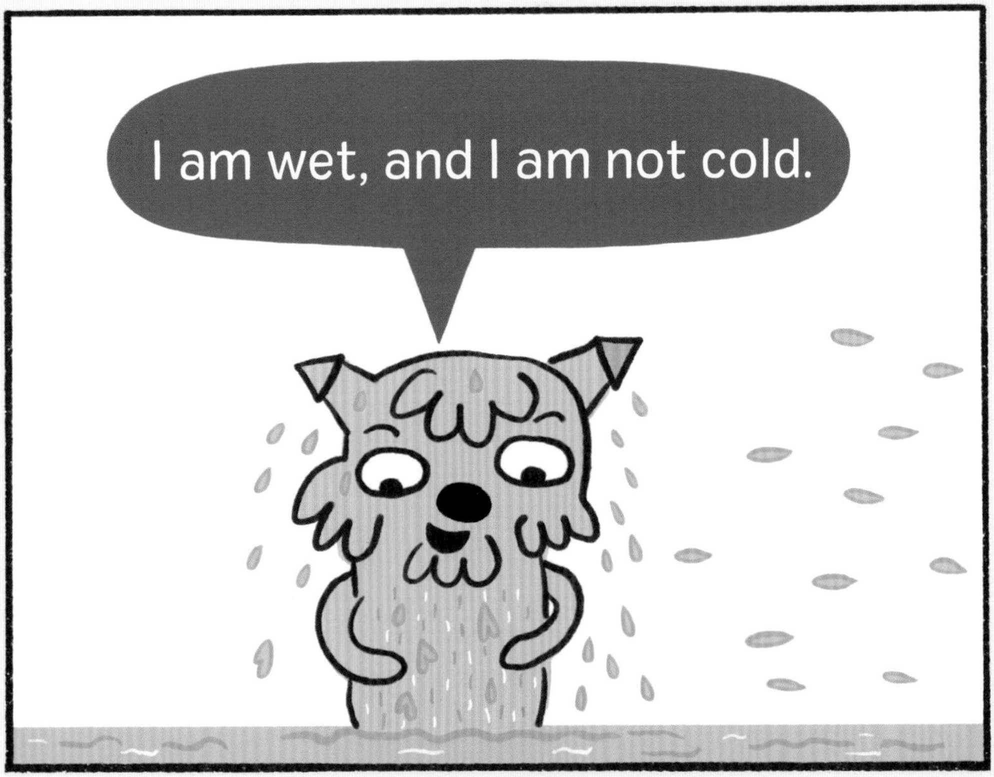
I am wet, and I am not cold.

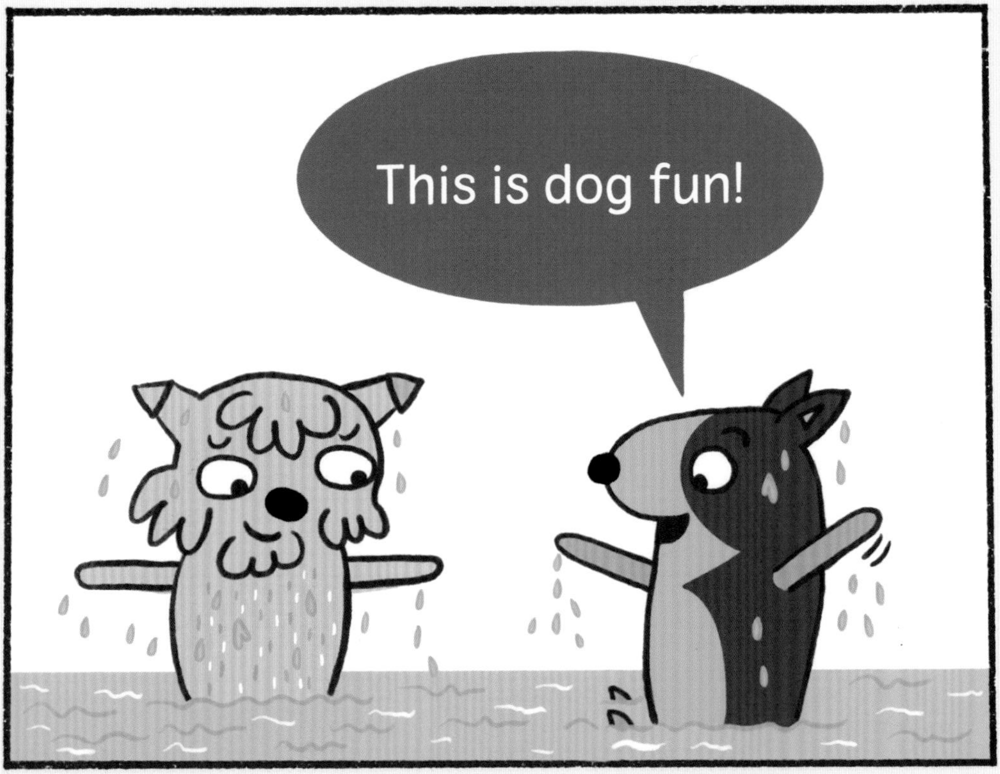
This is dog fun!

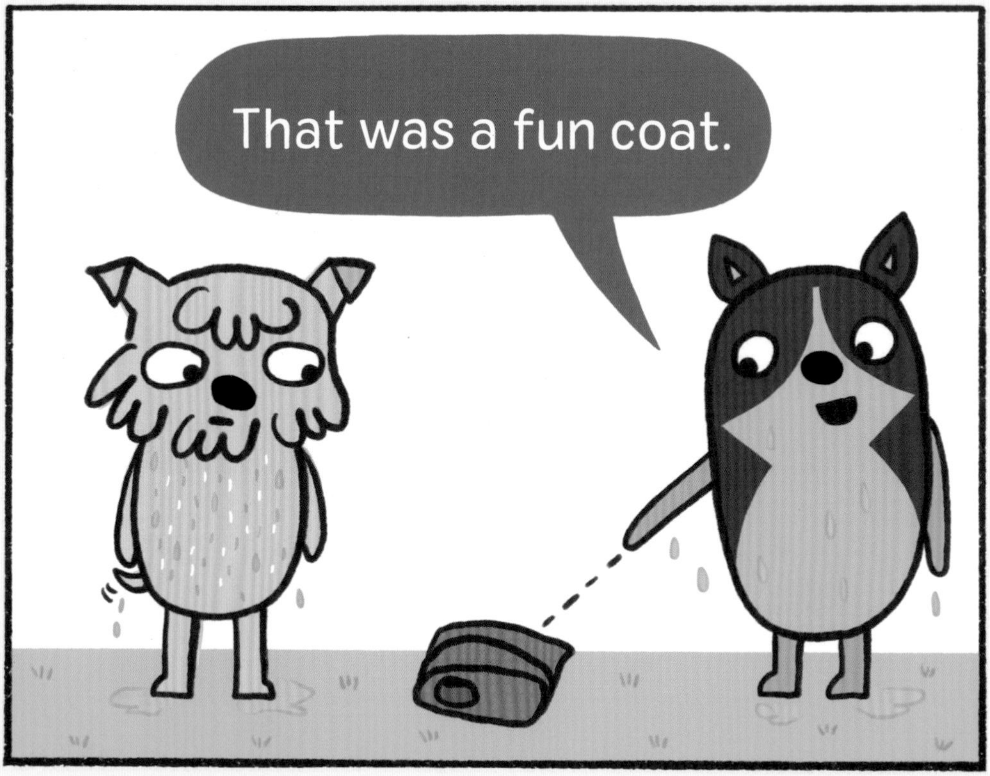
That was a fun coat.

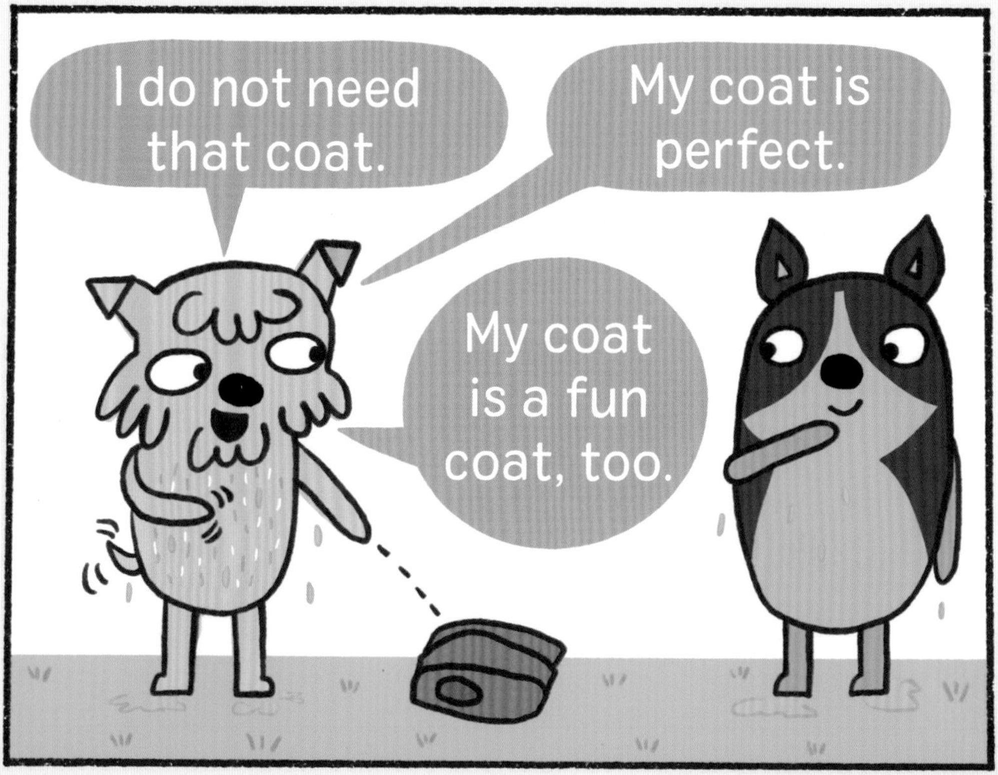
I do not need that coat.
My coat is perfect.
My coat is a fun coat, too.

Last cat question. Is cat fur good for puddles?

YES

NO

BUT...

that was puddle trouble.

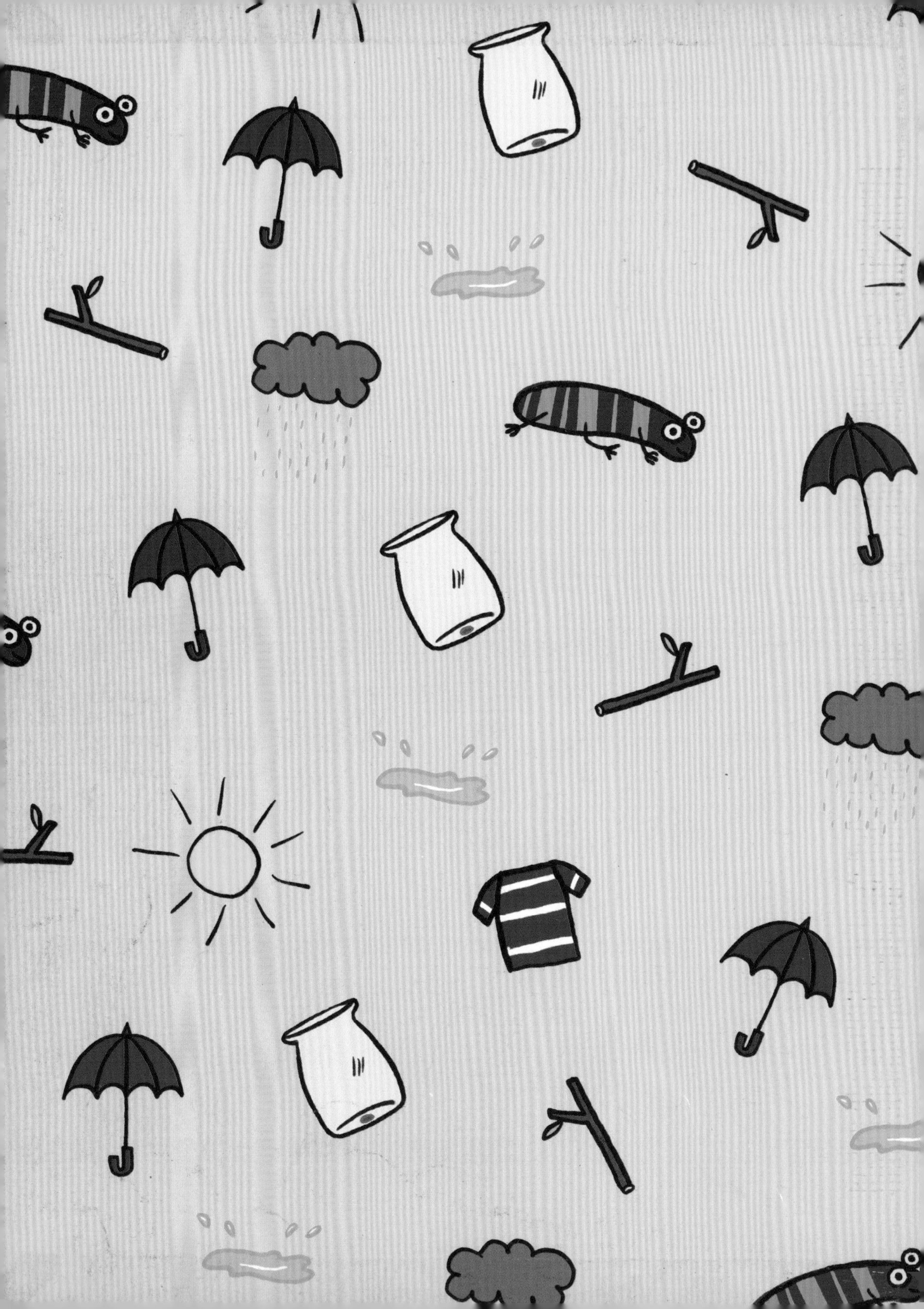